ISBN: 9798327237971

Ebook ASIN: B0DBR7TG3D

To My Darling Husband,

Thank you for illuminating my life in ways I never anticipated.

Til' A the Seas' gang dry

-L

CONTENTS

CHAPTER ONE

EDGAR

There are three truths you ought to know about Lilian Darling.

She is hopelessly reclusive, with little time for human interaction.

She knows more about witches than any person on the planet.

I absolutely and unequivocally adore her.

We reached our hotel as dusk began to settle around us. The journey had been long, and the thick mist and relentless rain had turned the expansive ten-acre landscape of our accommodation into a haunting blur of indistinct shapes poking from behind the hedge-lined road.

As the cab halted, the resort's imposing facade loomed into view. The red brick, vibrant in daylight, now appeared ghostly under the faint illumination spilling from the windows.

"That's Scotland for you," I mumbled.

The evening's oppressive gloom dashed our hopes for an after-dinner stroll through the historic grounds. As I exited the taxi, I wrapped my coat tighter around me, shivering. Despite the biting chill in the air, my body tingled with anticipation. The ancient buildings and cobbled pathways hummed with secrets; their timeless legends indifferent to the cold.

I tilted my head skyward to the mansion's towering upper stories before turning to face the expansive gardens. Beyond the parking lot and over a waist-high fence lay Dryburgh Abbey. The stone ruins stood like silent guardians. In the dim light, the crumbling walls etched with centuries of history disappeared into the obsidian void of night.

"Eerie," I murmured into the stormy night, a sudden chill coursing through me like ice water down my spine.

Lilian's voice cut through my reverie. "Ahem." Her fingers tapped on her small gold watch as she rotated her wrist to show me its face.

6:55. Our dinner reservation was for 7:00. Her jaw tightened; she despised tardiness, even a hint of it. Arriving fifteen minutes early was her unwritten rule, and we were cutting it close.

I flung a longing glance toward the abbey, but Lilian shifted again, her foot tapping an impatient rhythm against the cobblestones. With a sigh, I fell in tow behind her, passing through the archway and into the hotel's embrace.

The lobby welcomed us with a warmth that sharply contrasted with the wet world outside. An impressive chandelier cast a soothing twinkle over the polished wood and rich interior fabrics. A worn plaid carpet sprawled across the tiled floor, soaking up the rainwater dripping from our shoes.

Lilian approached the concierge to confirm our room, and then we shuffled to the restaurant, our steps sluggish with the added burden of damp clothes clinging to our skin.

6:58 p.m. "Whew." She wiped her brow, and her shoulders fell into a neutral position. We made it in the nick of time.

A bubbly hostess greeted us, her white shirt neatly buttoned to her chin.

"Reservation?" she inquired in a chipper tone.

"Darling, for two, for seven," said Lilian.

"Aye, cutting that one close!" the girl commented in the carefree sing-song accent of the Scottish Borders. Lilian shot me a look, and I gave a weak shrug as we trailed behind her bouncing ponytail weaving through a maze of polished tables alive with animated conversations.

Accents from all over mingled in the air, creating a vibrant symphony of culture. The hostess stopped with a practiced halt and gestured to a table nestled in the back corner of the dining room. Positioned in front of a large window, it offered a panoramic view of the abbey beyond, its hallowed silhouette looming against the foggy backdrop.

"Could we have that one instead?" Lilian purred, her voice dripping out ripe and sweet as she pointed to the far side of the room. "I'd prefer a riverscape while we eat." The corners of her mouth turned up in a strained, mechanical smile. The server, missing my raised eyebrows at Lilian's unusual tone, pranced with the eager enthusiasm of a golden retriever toward our new seat.

I knew why she did it. On a good day, keeping my focus was a challenge, but it would be impossible within sight of the abbey.

Sometimes, I think, Lilian knows me better than I know myself.

We sat across from one another and peeled off our waterlogged jackets. Lilian, pretending patience, waited while I surveyed the dining room, absorbing the hustle and bustle with glee until our server returned.

"What shall it be?" asked the young man.

"What do you recommend?" I asked.

"Well... the trout is particularly good and..."

Lilian cut in.

"Chef's pie for both of us, and two glasses of water."

I chuckled quietly, fully aware that I was getting under her skin simply for the fun of it. Her meal times were as rigid as every other aspect of her life. We had pored over the menu before even setting foot in the restaurant because it made her feel more at ease. We had independently chosen the pie, but the server eyed me wearily.

"That'll be all for now" I said with an assuring smile, and he trotted off to the kitchen, perplexed by the interaction.

"So, can we begin?" Lilian's words cut out, direct and sharp.

"That sounds more like you," I said with a wink as she pulled a thick, coil-bound notebook and a stack of research papers from her leather briefcase, each document covered in neon-green highlights.

She settled in front of the paperwork, aligning the sheets with precision and ensuring no single paper was out of place. As she opened her mouth to speak, I jumped in.

"Our itinerary," I said with a smirk.

She shot a disgruntled eyeroll in my direction as she flipped to page one. "If you order dessert, which I expect you to do, dinner will last until 8:30. We'll be in bed by 9:00, giving us eight hours of sleep before the 7:00 a.m. alarm tomorrow."

"Breakfast is at 7:30—"Our server appeared with our meals, hesitating as he searched for a spot amid her piles of papers. Lilian's face warped in frustration.

She shifted to the left, shielding her papers from the boy and creating a small space for a dish on the right. She slid the food away, determined not to eat until her overview was complete. Lacking such restraint, I pierced my fork into the flaky pie crust, my attention flickering between the savory flavors and her plan.

"As I was saying, breakfast is at 7:30. I am well aware that mornings aren't your thing; in fact, you tend to be a bit unbearable before 8:00 a.m., so you may skip it. At 8:00, I have a meeting with a source." Her words trailed off, an unusual hint of uncertainty creeping in.

This wasn't like her at all.

I looked up from my plate, piled high with brown gravy and succulent bits of meat, and locked eyes with her.

She cleared her throat and shifted in her seat. "I thought... you could take those two hours to explore the abbey. I should be able to manage the interview; you can meet me in St. Boswells at 10:00 a.m."

I inhaled sharply, causing a lump of pie crust to lodge in my windpipe. My coughing fit drew the attention of nearby diners and our server, who rushed over with jerky, uncertain movements, unsure if I required the Heimlich maneuver.

Lilian's lips compressed into a slender line. She waved off the confused young man and nudged my water toward me. I took a long swig, the cold liquid dislodging the mass, and cleared my throat.

"Lilian... tours always come last if there's time. Assignment first... we have deadlines... success comes from hard work... commitment to the cause is vital. That's what you've told me—every time we are on one of these godforsaken trips and I want to explore instead of tackling whatever historical side quest the university has sent us on."

"Of course, that's all still true," she replied, "but this time I'm making an exception. The person I'm meeting insisted I come alone. So rather than assigning you some project you are just going to moan about, I'm trying to be flexible in my approach and offer you the opportunity to do something you may actually enjoy."

Her mouth twitched, the corners lifting a bit. To most, it would look like an involuntary movement, a tick from which they would avert their eyes, but I knew it was her version of a smile. I shook my head and returned a much broader, toothier grin.

"You never cease to surprise me, Mrs. Darling," I said, raising my water glass to her. She gave a small, satisfied chortle and we finished our dinner in silence, just as she preferred.

Chapter Two

Curled in bed an hour later, the rhythmic patter of rain on the windowpanes lulled me into relaxation. My thoughts drifted back to Lilian's sly smile from earlier, a grin that always warmed me. Most people saw her as cold and uncompromising, but I knew the considerate, witty, and passionate person beneath her complicated exterior.

In the stillness of the night, her snoring reverberated through the room. She always slept the same way: flat on her back, eyes covered, and earplugs in. Her meticulously regimented sleep routine ensured the moonlight filtering through the sheer curtains wouldn't disturb her. Her system operated best with seven to eight hours of rest, and she had constructed this ritual to ensure she got it.

We had been on these trips together for five years now, and I had grown accustomed to her vampire-like evening drill, though I must admit it had frightened me initially. From our first study trip to the south of France, we had always shared a room. That night, as I watched her prepare for bed, I couldn't help but chuckle. I had foolishly taken her invitation to share a room as a sign of romantic interest. But as she moved about with mechanical precision—smoothing the covers until they were impeccably flat, checking the taps for even the slightest drip—it dawned on me that I might have been mistaken. The notion stung a bit, but there was something oddly endearing about her ritual, a far stretch from the sensual scenario I had envisioned.

My suspicions were confirmed as she finally slid between the sheets of her own bed.

"Edgar," she sighed, eyeing me with suspicion. "We have a duty and responsibility to utilize our donors' funds to further the understanding of history. Please don't misconstrue my request to share a room as anything more than a fiscally responsible decision to uphold the integrity of our work."

"Of course, Lilian. I'd never think it was more," I replied, settling across from her on the tiny twin cot, my ego only a tiny bit bruised.

By the end of that first trip, I learned that this was not meant to damage me; it was just how it was. In Lilian's world, relationships were mere wisps of things she had long ago abandoned. Family ties were severed years before, and social networks dissolved into oblivion. Then came me. In her solitary universe, I emerged as a singular entity of significance, disrupting the seclusion she had grown accustomed to. Her allowing me into her personal bubble was her form of intimacy, a rare opening of her guarded heart to another soul.

I rolled onto my side and admired her sleeping figure. She was quirky, and she embraced it. I envied her unapologetic approach to her lifestyle—a quality that set her apart from everyone else. Her individuality shone through in everything she did, and it was one of the many reasons I was drawn to her—though she wasn't always drawn to me.

When our paths first intersected in a collision of clumsy words and nervous laughter, friendship seemed unlikely. Yet, as fate would have it, an unbreakable bond was formed from those uncertain beginnings. I rolled away, aware that my admiring eyes could disturb her slumber. While she did her darndest to drown out the world so she could rest, that woman's brain was forever in overdrive. My eyes returned to the window as the memory of our first meeting unfolded in my mind.

When I accepted tenure at Oxford University, I was "warned" about Lilian Darling. Her name drifted through the corridors like a secret, opinions of her exchanged in hushed tones.

In department meetings—that she never attended—colleagues swapped glances and whispered behind their hands whenever Lilian was mentioned. At the faculty pub, in the private corners where the lights were dim, there were often voices dripping with intrigue and chuckling as they recounted how Lilian once recoiled from a simple handshake, as if the touch burned her—much like a witch.

The idea of Lilian being a witch was, of course, absurd. Her expertise in the Scottish witch trials was unparalleled, yet she dealt strictly with facts and truths; she embraced an air of cynicism when it came to mysticism. I should know—I had read all of her research. She possessed a rare gift for discernment, peeling back the layers of history with a precision that few, if any in the field could match. Her knack for analysis bordered on the supernatural, but that didn't justify the rumors. In her capable hands, many forgotten souls accused of witchcraft found redemption. Their stories were resurrected from obscurity, giving their memories a chance to reclaim their rightful place in the annals of history. Without her efforts, countless people would have been lost to time, their truths buried forever under the weight of injustice.

In those early days, I longed to meet her, yet there was a hint of truth in the mythos surrounding Lilian. Her presence was always tantalizingly out of reach.

Despite our offices being across the hallway from one another, she remained a specter. She vanished when her undergraduate class ended, leaving only an empty auditorium. Silence reigned supreme in her office, with not a flicker of movement. The room seemed frozen in time, untouched. Sometimes, I caught myself questioning her very existence.

Then, two years ago, my luck changed thanks to the Dean, who yanked her from her hiding place for an obligatory university event.

On that fateful evening, the grand hall of the Sheldonian Theatre buzzed with anticipation as philanthropists gathered to bestow their generosity upon our history department. Faculty members, dressed in their finest, paraded like prized stallions, each jockeying for the attention and favor of potential donors who handed over checks with feigned altruism, the tax benefits tallying behind their polished smiles. The air crackled with ambition. Amid the extravagant displays of ego, Lilian, a scholar of renown whose name carried influence in academic circles, sat in a far corner, content to linger out of the spotlight. Her appearance defied conventional beauty standards: a perpetual scowl marred her dainty lips, and her large chocolate eyes were set too close to the jagged bridge of her nose. Her mousy hair was cropped short in a pragmatic style. In a beige pantsuit that matched the wall behind her, she blended seamlessly into the background, a chameleon—nearly undetectable to the casual observer.

Yet, she was the only thing in the room I could see.

Spotting her in her hideout, I quickened my pace, weaving through the jockeying masses and inflated egos in her direction. Her piercing eyes locked onto mine as I drew nearer, then darted toward the door. I could see the wordless calculation, gauging the closing window of opportunity for escape before I reached her. She slumped in surrender as she realized our encounter was inevitable.

"Dr. Darling," I gushed, extending my hand. "My name is Edgar Falkirk, I work across the hall. I've been looking forward to meeting you."

Lilian's eyes flicked away, avoiding contact. My hand hovered midair, unshaken.

"I know," she said, her voice high-pitched and youthful.

"I've read all of your works, and I must say..."

"You've been stalking me," she snapped.

My jaw dropped open as I lowered my hand to my side.

"No, Dr. Darling, I haven't been stalking you. Our offices are next door to each other…"

She interrupted, cutting sharply through my defense. "Tuesdays and Thursdays at precisely 3:15, fifteen minutes after my undergraduate Scottish Witch-Hunting course ends, you can be found wandering outside my classroom."

A brush of irritation painted my face.

"Every afternoon at 4:00, as my office hours end, you always wander the hallway without purpose."

I expanded my chest, my nostrils flaring as I braced myself to proclaim my innocence.

"And last but not least," she said through gritted teeth, "you press your ear against my door to catch any sounds from inside."

"How did you know?" I murmured, mouth agape.

"Edgar Falkirk, shadows exist… and your feet cast them."

Her patience exhausted, Lilian stood and began to float toward the exit.

A surge of heat flushed my cheeks, and I clenched my fists. I glanced at her, my mind replaying the admiration I'd held for her work. This meeting had spiraled into a mess, nothing like I'd envisioned.

In a moment of reckless abandon, I shouted—my rebuttal ringing louder than intended through the room. A defiant echo of my wounded pride.

"Dr. Darling, I'm not stalking you, and I understand what shadows are... I just forgot about them." The instant the words left me, regret billowed through me, drowning my thoughts in an overwhelming flood.

The human mind—an intricate labyrinth of thought and reason—holds within it the potential for both brilliance and betrayal. No amount of education or refinement can shield you from its nature. I stuttered at the stupidity that had spewed from my lips.

I prayed my outburst would go undetected by my colleagues, but I couldn't be so lucky.

A collective disapproval trickled through the room as all attention turned to me. In the hallowed halls of academia, where intellect reigns supreme, there is a particular morbid fascination in witnessing the idiocy of one's peers laid bare for all to see. I had become the unwitting star of this impromptu spectacle, my own inadequacies on full display for the world to witness.

The heat of embarrassment burned deep, intensifying the crimson hues that stained my cheeks. My heartbeat pounded like a drum, each thud reverberating through my skull, a relentless reminder of my humiliation. Desperate to liberate myself from the spotlight of scrutiny, I prayed for the ground to swallow me whole. "God, kill me now, spare me the agony," I whimpered.

As I stood, havering, Lilian had pivoted, and for the first time, I witnessed her grin playing on her lips.

She sauntered back toward me as onlookers stared. Their leers fixed and unblinking, jaws hanging slack as they watched.

She was so close that I could see the gold flecks dancing in her dark eyes, sparkling only for me. I could count the tiny freckles sprinkled over the bridge of her nose. As she leaned in her voice dropped to a whisper, drawing me closer so that the faint aroma of her perfume, a delicate blend of lilac and lily, full-bodied and feminine, invaded my senses.

"Your name is Edgar Falkirk. Your office is across the hallway, and you are an expert in British folklore. I've read your works. They are rather insightful. You know what shadows are, and you are not a stalker. I was attempting to joke. It's not something I'm particularly good at. I possess something you may find interesting. I will deliver it to you tomorrow."

She turned on her heel and left.

A buzz of excitement electrified the room as onlookers exchanged eager whispers and speculative glances, weaving a web of gossip and theories about what she had said:

"Likely put a hex on him."

"That's why you leave her be."

"Well, you can't say you didn't warn him..."

I hid my face in my hands. After my clumsy display of ineptitude, the idea of mingling and discussing my academic achievements felt pointless. My already meager ego had deflated like a balloon, so I made for the exit too.

Lilian kept her promise.

The following day when I arrived at my office, a plump brown envelope awaited me, carefully slid under the door. It was feather-light, and a handwritten note in elegant cursive graced the front:

"An intriguing take on the existence of shadows."

I retrieved a pair of cotton archival gloves from my desk and slipped them on. Anticipation prickled the hairs on the back of my neck as I peeled back the layers of wrapping, revealing the treasure beneath.

Time had taken its toll on the document—its once pristine white sheen was now tinged with the muted hue of aged yellow. The vibrant ink had dulled, but the handwritten script was still legible when held to the harsh glare of the fluorescent light overhead. A delighted chuckle escaped my lips; it was a poem:

The Brollachan

Fae th' darkness, he appears.

Existing sin th' dawn o' years.

He bides tae roam th' hielan Moores.

In search o' souls, he kin transform.

Weary folk, please, marc mah heed.

*Brollachan appears as
they in need.*

*Fae shadows born thay
come tae ye.*

*Seeking shelter aye tis
true.*

*Bit warmth 'n' fairn
wull nae soothe their
soul.*

*Your body mortal thay
wull control.*

*Be wary folk o' th' fall o'
light.*

Fur Brollachan roam in
th' shadow o' nicht.

Below the verse lay a sketch, a series of black lines so laboriously etched onto the paper that the indentation pushed through on the reverse side. The ink strokes formed a childlike silhouette with two white circles and a crescent moon, creating a devilish smile. Below the drawing, the signature was illegible; its loops and curves diminished with time, except for the date 1532.

A sunburst of warmth blossomed in my chest. Lilian—the same Lilian who was so cold and calculated less than twenty-four hours before—had gifted me an original poem based on the lore that had consumed my academic pursuits for the last ten years.

I wrapped the gift with care and cradled it under my arm as I made my way across the hall. As I reached Lilian's door, my hand wavered in mid-air, snagged in a moment of uncertainty. Just then, the door swung open, and I jerked back, startled by the sudden movement.

"Come in," Lilian beckoned, expressionless as she ushered me into her office. Her space was a sanctuary of knowledge and order. Every surface gleamed with rich cherry wood, and the exterior walls overflowed with shelves of books, each one carefully color-coded to create a stunningly organized rainbow. She gestured to two wingback chairs, where she had placed a steaming pot of tea and two dainty China cups.

"Tea?"

"Yes, that would be lovely," I said, sitting stiffly in the chair and holding up the gift.

"Lilian, this is such a kind gesture," I began.

"Edgar, I feel as though I should explain myself," she interjected.

The unexpected interruption startled me, but I let her continue.

"First, I would like to apologize if my sense of humor caused you any discomfort yesterday. Next, I owe you a bit of an explanation."

I crossed my ankle over my knee and blew on the hot tea.

"I have not intentionally been avoiding you. In fact, I find your perspectives on British folklore very intriguing. I know what people say about me—that I am cold and elusive.

However, I want you to understand that I find many parts of this job exhausting." She fidgeted in her chair, her fingers tapping a rhythm known only to her on its arm. "Those lectures—with the bright-eyed undergrads and the relentless onslaught of questions—I can barely drag myself out of the room when they're done. I have seen you waiting in the hallway, and I knew you wanted to talk, but conversation is the last thing I want after a long day of forced interaction."

A puzzled look crossed over my face.

"Why did you get into teaching then?" I asked, perplexed by her revelation.

"I got into research," she clarified. "This office is my sanctuary." She gestured around her. "Teaching is an unfortunate side effect that I must manage in order to do what I enjoy."

Noticing the storm clouds of confusion gathering in my eyes, she sailed on with her explanation.

"I struggle a lot with interactions, Edgar, and it can often lead to people misconstruing my actions as rude or off-putting."

"I don't think you're off-putting," I said sincerely.

"Yet." Her voice trembled, carrying the faintest quiver of sorrow. "Edgar, the truth is, I appreciate your attention to detail, and I believe that together we could do great work. This gift is a peace offering for my previous dreadful attempt at humor and an invitation to partner with me on conducting some studies into the legends and lore surrounding witch trials in Europe. Would that be of interest to you?"

I nodded with enthusiasm.

"Good. I think we will make an excellent team. But from now on, please knock. Your stalking is unsettling." Her quirky half-grin spread across her face.

From that moment forward, the two of us became inseparable.

CHAPTER THREE

As I stirred from sleep, a symphony of songbirds greeted me. Their melodies cascading through the open window, mingling with the crisp scent of morning.

Last night's rain had left behind a sky dotted with fluffy white clouds, so pristine they seemed painted by a master's hand as they drifted across an azure canvas.

Lilian's absence struck me immediately. I bolted upright. A glance at the clock showed 8:20 a.m. I had already frittered away precious minutes for my tour of the abbey.

Standing in front of the mirror, I tilted my neck downward to take in my full reflection. At six feet two inches tall, my height was the first thing most people noticed about me. My blond hair was cut short and had begun to whiten at the temples, which I blamed more on the research and less on my age. My blue eyes, bright and benevolent, were now marked by persistent, sagging bags, a testament to the sleepless nights and long journeys I had endured.

I rummaged through my duffel bag and pulled out a plaid shirt and a pair of worn jeans. The shirt's soft fabric slipped over my head, the familiar pattern a comfort. Buttoning it up, I couldn't help but recall Lilian's carefully tailored pantsuits—always crisp, always professional. Compared to her polished appearance, my attire was juvenile and sloppy. I ran a hand through my hair, attempting to tame it, but it fell back into its usual disarray. With a resigned sigh, I gave up.

"That'll do," I murmured, pushing the thought aside as I hurried out the door.

A short iron gate marked the entrance to Dryburgh Abbey. The once winding dirt road, lined with majestic birch trees and rhododendrons, had been modernized into a narrow concrete trail leading to a quaint gift shop.

Under Historic Scotland's care, the abbey now charges a modest fee for entry to aid in its preservation. I entered the compact one-room store, the aroma of fresh paper and the crisp tang of window cleaner suffocating in the tiny space. I exchanged six pounds for the freedom to wander the grounds all day then ventured forth, sidestepping the tangle of visitors wrestling with audio guides.

Inside the serene expanse of the property, birdsong created a harmonious tapestry of sound. Wildflowers carpeted the ground in a riot of color, their delicate blooms brushing against my ankles as I walked. Cherry blossom petals danced on the breeze, infusing the air like sweet confetti.

I strolled along, my steps light and unhurried, marveling at the space's timeless beauty. Centuries-old oaks stretched their gnarled branches toward the heavens, whispering tales of days gone by into the stillness. Dryburgh Abbey had been a beacon of splendor in its heyday, its warm pink sandstone gleaming in the sunlight. Now, the crumbled ruins bore the scars of its tumultuous past. The abbey had endured four separate invasions, each time ravaged by fire and destruction. Yet, amidst the wreckage, traces of resilience persisted in its weathered walls.

I stalled along the north wall, catching sight of the famed Merelles Board, its intricate grid partially hidden by the tall, dewy grass that dampened my socks. The game board, one of the abbey's main attractions, featured squares similar to a chessboard carved into ancient stone. I kneeled and ran my fingers over the worn lines, noting the grooves etched by countless hands over the centuries. How many had gathered here, their laughter and strategies mingling in the air, whiled away in playful competition within these hallowed grounds?

The chatter of a passing tour group snapped me out of my fantasy. They crowded around me, craning their necks to catch a glimpse of the relic. I stood and waved them forward with a resigned smile. "Go ahead," I said as they surged en masse, pushing me to the rear of the pack. An exasperated sigh escaped my lips as I brushed at the wrinkles on my shirt, pretending the crowd had caused them rather than my own neglect. With hands on my hips, I waited, hoping for an apology that never came. Eventually, I gave up and strode off in the opposite direction.

A quick glance at my watch showed 9:45 already! My heart played a sudden staccato—time was passing quickly,

"Shit!" I moaned, quickening my pace. I had one more must-see before meeting Lilian: the tomb of Walter Scott.

Sir Walter Scott, the undisputed titan of Scottish literature, lay buried on these grounds. As I approached the entryway, an archway adorned with intricate carvings framed the solemn site. The aroma of wet earth penetrated the air, interweaving with the faint perfume of wildflowers. A nearby plaque, its edges worn smooth by time, detailed Scott's monumental legacy and enduring impact on Scotland and beyond.

Leaning against the faded stone, I closed my eyes and let the quietude of the surroundings wash over me. The whispers of the past blended with the rustling leaves as I mouthed the words of Scott's haunting poem, "The Dance of Death."

"Yield we place to sterner game,
Ere deadlier bolts and direr flame
Shall the welkin's thunders shame,
Elemental rage is tame
To the wrath of man..."

The lumbering footsteps of an approaching visitor ruined the tranquility of my tribute. The tour group had caught up to me again. I turned on my heels, ready to defend myself from the oncoming throng, but as I turned, there was nobody there.

My brows knitted together as I surveyed the barren landscape surrounding me.

Rubbing my temples, I let out a slow exhale, feeling my neck and shoulders stiffen. I resumed my memorial, bowing again toward Scott's tomb, the cold monument pressing into my palms. But as soon as I closed my eyes, ready to continue, the rhythmic stomping returned, echoing off the antique walls.

"For Christ's sake!" I muttered through clenched teeth. I spun around, my eyes narrowing as they locked onto the source of the noise. My heart pounded against my ribcage.

Nothing.

I paused, straining to decipher the sound. The distant murmur of the tour group was now a background hum, almost drowned out by the pounding in my ears. The hair on the back of my neck stood on end as I scanned the surroundings, my breaths shallow and rapid.

Why did I hear them? Was I overtired? Hungry? Or had years of research driven me to insanity like so many before me? The possibilities swirled in my mind, each more unsettling than the last.

The echo of heavy footsteps replayed in my psyche, every thud still vivid. Had someone really been there?

Yes, I was confident. The sound had been too clear, too deliberate.

Should I tell Lilian I've begun hallucinating?

No, probably not.

As I conducted an internal psychological assessment, the sound resurfaced. It came from my left now, a constant rhythm crunching on the gravel path. Each footfall seemed to reverberate through the still air, growing fainter and quicker with every passing second.

Driven by a confrontational impulse to address the mystery walker, I stomped off in pursuit, weaving my way through the lusterless rows of deteriorating graves. I reached a steep embankment. Skidding to a halt, I peered down at the plunging creek below. The sight gave me pause, but the noise hammered an unrelenting rhythm in my ears, compelling me forward.

"Down we go," I panted, sliding down the hill and splashing feet-first into the murky abyss. "This better be worth it," I grumbled as cool water bubbled and swirled around my ankles. Each movement was a battle against an unyielding current. With determined focus, I navigated the rocky bed and scrambled up the opposite side.

Reaching the top, I scanned the horizon. Before me stretched a vast woodland where birch and oak trees mingled, their branches intertwining in a natural cocoon. A chain-link rope marked the abbey boundary. In the warm breeze, a weathered sign creaked, its faded letters whispering to visitors that they were exiting the grounds:

Private Property. No Entry Beyond This Point.

The clamor of steps reverberated from the pith of the grove, loud and ethereal, the sound ringing through the woodland.

I cast aside my lingering uncertainty and hoisted my right leg over the fence, followed by my left. Pausing, I strained my ears for any signal of alarm—a bark, a shout, the piercing wail of a siren. The seconds stretched on, but all was quiet, save for the rustle of leaves and the faraway chirping of birds. I took a deep breath and prepared to move.

Then, footsteps.

I bolted toward the noise.

The dense forest enveloped me in the earthy scent of wild onions, their delicate fragrance distinct and pungent against the humidity of the woodland air. The ground was blanketed with lush greenery, punctuated by bursts of white blossoms. Holly bushes clustered around the gnarled trunks of ancient oaks, their thorny boughs choking the bark.

Pushing through the tangles, I fought for every inch of forward progression as my legs snagged on the grasping undergrowth. My lungs burned, a sharp sting reminding me of my years of desk work and lack of physical prowess. Branches clawed at my skin, as if the trees themselves sought to impede my progress. Still, I forged ahead.

On the horizon I could see a break in the overgrowth where sunlight streamed through the darkness.

Then I saw them—not close enough to make out any distinctive attributes, but near enough to see their shadowy figure at the grove's edge.

Fixing my eyes forward, I urged my weary lungs to propel me onward. The silhouette stood unmoving, anticipating my approach.

"What do you want?" I yelled, my baritone voice trilling through the thicket like a drum as I crushed through the last of the vegetation and emerged into the grove.

The transition felt like crossing into another realm, the luminescence of the sunlight a stark contrast to the damp forest

I had just left behind. In the heart of the clearing, a near-perfect circle appeared, devoid of any trees or growth, as if nature had carved out this spot for a purpose.

The ground was firm and well-tended, hinting that someone, or something, took great pride in keeping this section of land clear. I stopped, bending over and battling the stabbing pang in my side.

"Hey! Why are you running?" I called out, my voice strained and breathless. My eyes lifted, tracing the path where the figure had stood moments before.

Gone.

"What... is happening?" I muttered, eyes darting along the tree line. I listened for any hint of movement, anticipating the rhythm of an approach.

Nothing.

Nobody.

Only me, alone with no signs of anyone, anywhere.

"What the actual..." A sudden noise cut through my curse—a familiar sound, yet oddly out of place: the rustling of paper.

I turned my head, searching for the source. Careful steps brought me to the spot where the shape had disappeared, and my senses sharpened.

In the void of the grove, something jutted from the earth. I squinted, willing my eyes to focus as I moved forward. A tall obelisk rose from the perimeter.

"How did I miss that?" I wondered, my historian's instincts sparking, my mind racing through possibilities. "It could be a hitching post," I said aloud. "Or..." I pondered. "It could also be a grave." My pulse quickened.

The rustling grew louder, the sound intensifying as I drew nearer until the stone stood before me, its lackluster surface beckoning. I reached out, my fingers brushing its rough texture, eroded by years of exposure. My skin prickled with an unseen chill, and a creeping sense of paranoia set in as I rescanned my environment for watching eyes.

"Calm down," I muttered to myself. "Nobody's here."

But I couldn't shake the nagging sensation that somewhere, someone was watching this scene unfold.

I straightened my back and slid my hands into my pockets—an attempt to look casual as I examined the obelisk from different angles. There were no identifying marks, no inscribed birthdates or loving testimonies to a person gone long ago. But the soil around its base squished under my feet with the soft erosion that often surrounds old burial sites.

Images surged through my mind of the ground falling away, and my courage evaporated. I stumbled back, my heel landing on something solid and raised as I did so.

I squeezed my eyes shut as the earth beneath me seemed to pulse. I bore down again, feeling the texture through my shoes. There was no crack or squish to suggest human remains, and I heaved a hulking sigh, swallowing a laugh at my own expense.

With newfound bravery, I lifted my shoe and looked down.

"What the...?" I frowned, bending to pick up my find.

Under my step lay a pocket-sized cowhide book. Moss clung to its cover, but it looked well-preserved, its rich caramel-brown colour and gold leaf lettering glistening in the sunlight.

Seilbh Iseabail Alasdair

Excitement snaked through me as my fingers glided over the cover's surface, savoring the intricate details with my touch. With each stroke, vivid images of mysterious stories danced in my mind, waiting to be unearthed from its pages.

RING RING RING

The detestable instrumental ringtone of my cellphone pierced the tense atmosphere. With a jolt, I retrieved the phone from my pocket.

10:05 a.m.

LILIAN

"Oh, shit," I exclaimed, fumbling with the buttons to answer.

"Hey, Lilian," I said, trying to sound relaxed while simultaneously bracing myself for the inevitable lecture about my tardiness.

"It's late. Are you okay?" Lilian's voice quivered with apprehension.

"I'm fine. I just got... turned around," I lied.

"Alright... good..." She paused. "I was worried."

A grin tugged at my lips, surprised by this rare display of tenderness from Lilian.

"I'll be there in twenty minutes," I reassured her and hung up, my cheeks flushing with warmth. Her words, unexpected and warm, enswathed me. At the same time, guilt churned in my gut for finding comfort in her concern. I slid the book into my jeans pocket, took a deep breath to fill my aching lungs, and braced myself for the long run back to the hotel.

Chapter Four

St. Boswells reminds me of a fairy tale, with its sandstone cottages and quaint shops nestled along a narrow, winding main street. Each house glows warmly, and the gardens overflow with foxgloves and wisteria, enhancing the magical experience. Once a prominent farming district, the community has evolved into an artistic enclave brimming with boutique stores and eateries. As one of the first stops on St. Cuthbert's Way—a historic trail connecting the abbeys of the Scottish Borders to Lindisfarne—the streets bustle with walkers starting their trip, their footsteps mingling with those of medieval pilgrims.

Navigating the bumpy streets in search of a parking spot, I smiled at the adventurers meandering through the downtown core. Their auras shone with energy and enthusiasm, undimmed after the initial twelve kilometers of their 100-kilometer trek. Backpacks hung loose on their backs, and their socks remained dry under the warm May sun.

The cab driver jostled to a stop, blocking the street and eliciting frustrated honks from oncoming traffic. I pulled a tenner from my pocket and thrust it into the front seat. "Keep the change," I said over my shoulder and hopped out.

Our meeting spot was a small but bustling café and bookshop, which had windows adorned with vibrant, hand-painted spring scenes of the Borders. A line of people wound out the door and around the corner. I squeezed through the throngs, muttering apologies, my eyes scanning the jam-packed venue for Lilian.

I brightened when I saw her sitting at a table near the window, her fingers tapping an intricate rhythm on the ceramic surface of an oversized coffee mug. As she spotted me weaving amongst the masses, relief washed over her face.

"I'm so sorry..." I began, then hesitated. My excuse would sound absurd to the logical Lilian. "I got lost on the abbey grounds."

Lilian's brow creased, her rebuttal lingering on her lips, before she shook off her concern and continued on.

"My lead," she said, shifting the conversation, "is a brilliant doctoral student at Aberdeen University. She's delving into the history of witchcraft in the Scottish Borders. Her research has zeroed in on one woman who faced trial multiple times. She tracked down the home where this woman lived. The place is undergoing extensive renovations, so the owners agreed to let her explore the site. She's been practically living there, overseeing every inch as the contractors peeled back layers of time. And just last week, they unearthed something extraordinary beneath the old flooring."

She slid a small piece of paper across the table, her hands unsteady. I picked it up and began to read:

"Transferal of Powers:

Whit's mines is yers', yers is mine, let oor powers cross the line, I offer up this gift to share and transfer powers thru thy air."

I glanced at her, seeking an explanation or reassurance, but her face was turned away, her mouth pressed into a thin line, and her skin had shed its usual luster.

"It's a…"

"Spell!" I interjected, my excitement clashing with Lilian's nervousness.

"It appears to be," she said, her eyes flickering with unease.

"This is preposterous," I said, turning the sheet over in my hands.

Lilian observed me, her body leaning forward. "It's from a book, Edgar."

"I don't understand."

"Look," she said, pointing to the margin of the paper where small perforations trailed like breadcrumbs. "It's been ripped, see?"

My hand brushed against my jeans, resting on the book in my pocket. Lilian's discovery captivated me so much that I had almost forgotten about my remarkable find. My fingers curled around the object, tracing its boxy shape. I was about to reveal my find when Lilian's urgent voice broke through.

"She was unsettling, Ed. When I suggested that page might belong to a book, she begged me to locate it. I said I'd try, but her reaction was beyond intense—borderline hysterical. It scared me."

Lilian's frightened words lingered, an invisible mass pressing down on me. I hated seeing her upset. As someone who usually brushed off odd behavior with ease, her distress was alarming. The woman she described had left her shaken, her usual composure replaced by tense, uneasy fidgeting. I could see how her fingers trembled as she held the paper, and the tightness around her eyes. Whatever had happened with that woman had rattled Lilian to her core. This wasn't like her. The realization hit me like a cold wave, and a protective urge surged. Something had disturbed her, and that thought alone was enough to set my pulse aflutter.

"She's excited, Lilian. You, more than anyone, know what it's like to be on the verge of a breakthrough that could validate all those grueling hours of study. We'll do everything we can to assist her," I said with a reassuring smile. I withdrew my hand from my pocket, and the thrill of my discovery ebbed away, replaced by a gnawing sense of dread. I had no idea who this woman was, but if she was erratic enough to unsettle Lilian, I had no desire to meet her.

Chapter Five

Three days.

Lilian had been poring over the pocket-sized piece of paper for three days, her stare boring into it like a missile. The room's light shifted from dawn to dusk as she flipped through endless archival records, her fingers moving with an agitated energy. Shadows under her eyes deepened with each unanswered question, her frustration etched into her furrowed brow.

On the third day, unable to bear her torment any longer, I retrieved the book from my bag. The ghost of the student who had made Lilian tremble lingered in my mind, but guilt, bitter and unrelating, was consuming me. I was hiding something that could spare her further suffering. If this was what she sought, it meant confronting the unsettling woman—a meeting I selfishly wanted to avoid.

But I couldn't be selfish anymore. Lilian's eyes, often shrewd and confident, were now clouded with doubt and exhaustion. Her hands shook from excessive caffeine as she turned another page. Even if this wasn't the solution, it might offer her a moment's respite from the relentless torment of her unsolvable case.

I approached her as she hovered over the desk in our hotel room, eyes fixed in a trance-like stare. My fingers glided over the intricate patterns on the cover, feeling the secret I'd been guarding in each swirl and flourish. Lilian seldom showed emotion, but keeping this from her may hurt her. The thought of disappointing her was an anchor dragging me down.

I swallowed hard, but the tightness in my throat refused to ease. "Lilian," I whispered.

She remained lost in her labyrinth of contemplation. I drew nearer and touched her elbow, the heat of her skin instantly cooled by my icy fingers.

"Lilian." She flinched, as if waking from a dream. "Lilian, there's something I need to tell you," I said, my voice uncertain. "And I understand if you're upset. Please believe me, I never intended to betray your trust." I paused, searching for the right words. "I didn't tell you because I didn't want to help the woman who unsettled you. But I found something in the woods beyond the abbey."

I handed her the treasure and her fingers brushed mine as she took it. The room seemed to hold its breath.

She turned the book over, tracing its cover with a delicate touch. The silence stretched, each second an eternity. She thumbed through the pages, her eyes widening with a spark of excitement. Suddenly, she lunged forward, her composed facade shattering. She wrapped her arms around my neck, tears streaming down her cheeks, not wrathful tears, but tears of pure, unadulterated joy. Every sob was a symphony of relief, resonating through the room and lifting the heaviness from my soul.

"You beautiful, remarkable man," she exclaimed. "You've found it!" Stunned, I stood rooted to the spot, my mind swirling with a torrent of emotions. Lilian and I shared a bond forged through conversations, parallel work, and quiet dinners. Physical touch had never been part of our kinship. In fact, this was the first time she had ever embraced me. My arms dangled like pendulums, searching for a place to rest. Slowly, I wrapped myself around her, surrendering to the rare moment of tenderness. I stood there basking in her affection, but only for a moment because Lilian stirred, her body growing rigid, and I reluctantly let go. She drew back, her focus shifting to the treasure cradled in her hands. She sat at the foot of the bed, her posture straight and determined, her eyes fixated on the find.

"Seilbh Iseabail Alasdair," she pronounced in Gaelic, the words rolling off her tongue with ease. "Well, we now have a name. It roughly translates to 'Property of Isobel Alexander.'"

She opened the book, her fingers tracing the seams as she turned the pages searching for a mark, any mark on the spine, that would confirm her suspicions: that the sheet she possessed had once belonged within.

"It does appear to be a grimoire of sorts—a succession of directives on folk magic, spells, and incantations. Did I tell you? Did the student mention the name of the woman she is researching? The one who vanished?" she asked, her eyes flicking up to confront me.

I shrugged. "Not that I recall."

"I find it hard to believe these two artifacts aren't connected," she continued, oblivious to my shift in mood. "There are too many similarities in content and location for it to be coincidental." Lilian's eyes narrowed and she tapped at her temples. "Based on the number of folk magic books that have been discovered—which is, to my knowledge, exactly zero, I think the probability of it being from another folk practitioner in the same village is exceedingly unlikely. I'll need to reach out to my source and clarify some details."

I rolled my eyes, frustration bubbling up inside me. In Lilian's world the strange woman was a crucial piece of the mystery whether she was unsettling or not. With a sigh that squealed like a deflating balloon, I flopped backward onto the bed, arms spread wide while Lilian hurried to the old white phone on the bedside table. She dialed quickly as if from memory and shifted from foot to foot as she waited for an answer.

"Lizzy," Lilian said into the receiver.

"Lizzy," I mimicked with a childlike lilt. "So, the mystery woman has a name."

"Lizzy, it's me," she said, more urgently. "Sorry to bother you, but I never got the name of the woman you were researching, the one who disappeared."

I leaned in, curiosity piqued as my ears strained to catch a response.

"Interesting, well, I think we should meet again. I've found something I believe you'll find quite compelling."

Lizzy's voice rose in urgency, her words crashing through the phone like a sudden downpour.

"I know you have questions, but we will discuss this in person. When are you...?"

Lilian's expressions changed quickly—furrowed brows, a sudden smile, a quick glance my way. My eyebrows shot up, hoping she'd clue me in.

"I see... Okay... We'll make it work," Lilian said, placing the receiver back with a deliberate click, no unnecessary farewells. She turned to me with a gleam in her eye. "We must meet her tonight, 7:00 p.m. at the Temple of the Muses."

A whine poured out of me, like a temperamental child.

"Before we go, though," she sputtered, her voice an equal blend of urgency and suspicion. "Can you brief me on how you found this book?"

I steadied myself and began, "I was on the abbey grounds and had gone to Scott's monument—"

"I love that monument... Did you know..." Lilian interjected; her enthusiasm effervescent. I shot her a glare, and she folded her hands in her lap.

"As I was saying, I had stopped at Scott's monument and was reciting 'The Dance of Death.'"

Lilian raised a finger, prepared to offer an interesting tidbit of information, but I shook my head and she slumped back.

"I was interrupted by footsteps, but when I turned around nobody was there. It happened three more times. I got annoyed and followed the sound. It led me off the property and into the woods, where an old monument stood. The book was lying at the foot of the monument."

She studied my face, searching for any hint of facetiousness.

"Let me get this straight," she said, placing her hands under her chin. "You followed a strange silhouette into the forest and stumbled upon a stone and an ancient spellbook?"

"That's pretty much it," I said defensively.

"You... Edgar Falkirk, who wrote your entire thesis on the Brollachan, a mischievous shape-shifting shadow monster who lures people to their demise, WILLINGLY followed some creature into the unknown?"

I slouched, pressing my pointer fingers to my lips. "I suppose I did... but Lilian, the Brollachan is folklore, a story to scare children into staying close to home. It's not real."

She hesitated, her eyes flicking to the moss-covered book resting open on the bed. "Until three days ago, I would have agreed... Now, I'm not so sure."

Chapter Six

The Temple of the Muses was a short stroll from the hotel. Despite Lilian's usual reluctance towards exercise, she nodded with enthusiasm when I suggested we walk. The discovery of the book had clearly shaken her, and my account of how I found it rattled her even more. As we started our journey, I stifled a laugh as she scurried along, her usually robotic movements now fluid and unsteady.

Lilian had always approached the Witch Trials with a pragmatic mindset, believing in rational explanations for all accusations. The notion of legitimate witchcraft had never entered her mind. Yet, here we were, with a book that suggested at least one "witch" might have practiced some form of folk magic.

Her unease was evident as she flailed down the path, recounting the eccentric history of the grounds on which we trekked with the fervor of a tour guide.

"All the land around us, including the abbey ruins, once belonged to the Earl of Buchanan," she said, sweeping her arms wide to encompass the vast landscape. "He was a peculiar man, by all accounts. He treasured Scotland and its history, and many of the features you see were created as tributes to Scotland and its lore."

Her voice carried on the wind as I nodded along, captivated by her tale.

"Originally, the Temple of the Muses was his personal tribute to James Thomson's 'The Four Seasons,'" Lilian said, her eyes brightening. "It began as a nine-pillared rotunda with a carving of Apollo atop a pedestal, crowned with laurel wreaths. The pedestal also featured detailed carvings of the nine muses."

I jogged to keep up with her energetic pace.

"Each pillar had metallic engravings of the muses' names. It was a marvelous place in its prime, but it fell into disrepair over time. The monument to Apollo and the engravings were removed, leaving only the base, which nature reclaimed. In 2002, a local artist was commissioned to restore the statue inside the structure, leading us to where we are today." Lilian motioned to the display before us, her storytelling reaching a crescendo. My mouth tumbled open at the sight before us.

The Four Seasons stood as a haunting substitute for the old Apollo. Though I had never seen the original, I preferred this version. Weathered green by exposure, the bronze statue depicted four nude women embracing in a circle.

We climbed the grassy hill to where the monument perched. The women's faces bore complex expressions, their hands resting on one another with tenderness and devotion, supporting each other's evolution through life. Lilian's lips quivered, a subtle smile forming as she monitored my amazement. I ran my fingers over the aged ore of the statues, relishing in the bumpy texture under my fingertips.

"I adore it," I said, a radiant glow spreading across my face.

"I knew you would," she replied, her eyes twinkling.

Our serene moment was obliterated as a stinging voice sliced through the tranquil atmosphere. The woman I had hoped to avoid appeared at the bottom of the hill, her presence sending chills down my spine. She was tall and thin with dark hair that cascaded down her back like a waterfall. Her cheekbones could cut glass and her pastel blue eyes pierced through me. Her pouty lips, a vibrant shade of maroon, curved slightly as if holding back a secret.

She was a vision and a nightmare, and I jumped at the sight of her.

"Lilian!" she bellowed from below, her cry cutting through the surrounding landscape and startling nearby pigeons into frightened flight.

Lilian managed a feeble wave in response as Lizzy ascended the hillside. Before she even reached us, her shrill voice fired off a rapid succession of questions, each one scraping against my patience.

"Did you find something? Did you find a book? Where did you find it?" she demanded.

Lilian raised a hand to calm her. "I found something, Lizzy," she said, her demeanor steady amidst the tension. "But first, we need to come to an understanding about the information I'm about to share."

Lizzy nodded, her eyes aflame, her dagger-like fingernails clicking together like a child eager to unwrap a gift. I moved away and perched myself on the monument's edge, tracing patterns in the soil with my foot.

"We found a book," Lilian said anxiously. "It appears to have belonged to the woman you are researching and contains what I can only describe as folk magic."

"Where?" Lizzy commanded.

"Near the abbey. Did the woman you're studying have any connection to the abbey?"

"She lived in the area—maybe she helped with the gardens, let me see it," she demanded, her skeleton-like hands reaching out for the book.

I glanced over my shoulder and saw Lilian scuffle backwards. I tensed and moved toward them, squaring my shoulders and lengthening to my full height. "You'll see it Lizzy, but first, please answer her questions. She can help you sort this out, but you need to—"

"Who are you?!" Lizzy interrupted, her razor-sharp fingernails jabbing at my chest like talons. Lilian protectively moved in front of me, though I could still see Lizzy's icy features glaring at me over the top of Lilian's head.

"This is my colleague, Edgar," she announced, her voice firm. "Show some gratitude—he's the one who found your book. I am giving it to you," Lilian said, extending the book toward Lizzy. "But I hope that you will take a look and then allow me to have it for a day or two to make some archival copies."

Lizzy seized the book, her eyes bulging. She flipped it open, put her nose into the bindings and sniffed, relishing its age-old secrets. She then turned to the side and murmured to herself, as if drawn by some unseen energy. She quickly flipped through the pages with eerie intensity, finally stopping toward the back of the book, where her fingertips traced the words inked on the page. A malevolent glint sparked in her eyes, and a twisted sneer curled her lips into a grotesque grin. Before our horrified eyes, she began to sway on her feet, her movements growing frenzied. Her body erupted into convulsions, each spasm wracking her frame.

"Are you alright, Lizzy?" Lilian asked, her voice quaking.

"Lilian, my dear Lilian," Lizzy rasped, "I've searched for this for so long, and now you've found it. I knew I could count on you. You are a gem."

She held the book high above her as her muscles contracted and relaxed in rapid succession. Her back arched in a sickening inverted fold as her head snapped backward, then forward, then side to side.

"Lilian… I have a bad feeling about this. What is happening?"

Lilian raised her hand, gesturing for quiet as the realization dawned on her. Her face became an alabaster mask, contorted by creeping dread.

"Edgar… It's a spell… She's doing a spell. Edgar, get the book!"

We both lunged forward, desperation fueling our movements as we tried to tackle Lizzy and stop her incantation. My arms locked around her shins as suffocating darkness descended upon us, the sky blackening as if midnight had landed at midday. The inky abyss engulfed me before I even felt the impact.

I saw nothing.

Heard nothing.

Felt nothing.

There was only black.

Chapter Seven

A biting ache in my temples jolted me awake, shooting through my skull like a thousand needles piercing my brain. I coerced my eyes open, blinking as I waited for the haze to disband. Above me in the sky loomed great grey clouds leaden with the promise of rain.

I was not in my bed.

As my vision sharpened, vivid memories of Lizzy and our bizarre encounter surged over me like an unstoppable tide. Each recollection crashing with monstrous waves of uncontrollable anxiety.

"Lilian," I called out, my voice breaking mid-syllable.

No response.

"Lilian, where are you?" My chest tightened as invisible talons squeezed me, restricting my breath.

The silence was deafening.

"Lilian, I need you..." I gulped, swallowing hard, then corrected myself. "I need you to answer me."

A faint out-of-the-way voice responded, "I'm here."

"Oh thank God," I said to myself as relief washed over me like a cool breeze, loosening the knot of anxiety coiled around my insides.

The heavens finally opened and the first raindrops pattered down to the earth. The water stung my eyes, blurring my vision, but I couldn't bring myself to rise. I blinked slowly, struggling to make sense of my surroundings through the slit of sky above me.

Once more I closed my eyes, then opened them.

Lilian's outline hovered over me, her neat pantsuit clinging to her body and glistening with mud. Pine needles stuck out from her tangled hair, and a nasty bruise mottled the skin around her eyes, which were wild with terror.

"Are you okay?" she asked, extending her hand to help me.

"I... I think so," I stammered as I scrambled to my feet. "Your eyes," I murmured, reaching out to caress the purple bruises on her face. She winced and turned away.

"I tried to grab you when you fell, but it got so dark. I think I hit something when I landed," she said, running her fingertips carefully over her distended eye socket.

We stood there shivering, surveying our surroundings as rain cascaded down our drenched bodies, blending with the grime and debris clinging to our skin. Then, in a moment thick with anticipation, Lilian drew in a deep, shaky breath.

"...I..."

"You there!" A gravelly voice interrupted Lilian and I spun around toward the call.

From beyond a tangle of trees, a man emerged, striding purposefully at us. His fiery red hair was cropped short, framing a prominent forehead that jutted out like a rocky cliff. His cheeks were pitted with scarring, and his lips were chapped and thin. His solid, oak-like frame loomed over us, making me shrink back as I looked up. He must have been at least six foot five.

"What are ya doin'? Who are you?" he bellowed, his hoary Scottish drawl thundering outward like a cannon.

Lilian's response shot out like an arrow. "Lilian! I'm Lilian Darling, and I'm afraid I'm lost." The sound of Lilian's English accent caused the stranger to halt in his tracks, frozen like a deer in headlights. He folded his mammoth arms over his chest, the muscles tense against the skin.

"Where did ya come from?" he inquired.

I tapped at my pockets in search of my ID—my wallet was gone. "We are professors. We work at Oxford University," I replied, my voice wavering. "We are in Scotland doing research."

His brow furrowed, deepening the dimpled scars on his face. "Doin' what?! From where?!"

"Oxford! Oxford University!" I bellowed, hoping the sheer volume would bridge the barrier between us.

My raised voice acted like a siren call, drawing a small army out of the woods. Each man carried rudimentary tools, dragging them along the forest floor with a rhythmic scrape. They gathered around the red-headed figure, their voices low and conspiring as they exchanged furtive glances in our direction.

"Who is that?" asked one of the men, who was short and round like a human barrel.

"I am unsure," answered the redhead. "They claim to hail from Oxford, a woman… from Oxford," he sneered, his gaze lingering on Lilian. His eyes scanned her like a predator zeroing in on its target and I stepped forward, placing myself in front of her to shield her from his leers.

"English, are ya?" the stout man inquired.

"Yes, clearly!" I retorted, my voice edged with frustration. "We are lost! We are here studying. Can you please tell us how to get to the Dryburgh Hotel?"

Their murmurs swelled into a crescendo as they drew nearer, forming a compact ring, their heads bowed in solemn deliberation.

"Never heard of it," said the burly redhead.

"Christ Almighty," I hissed. "It's not here. We are trying to get there! It's a big red brick house next to Dryburgh Abbey;

you can see the ruins from the parking lot! Can you tell us how to get there?"

The men's jittery interjections and feverish whispers swirled together until they reached a frenzied roar. The redhead fought to rein in his unruly comrades, his attempts at control crumbling. The atmosphere was thick with the heat of their escalating anger. Then, the stout man lumbered forward.

"You're here ta' desecrate our abbey? Haven't you English done enough damage?" As he spoke, his tone grew lower and more menacing. A dark flush crept across his pudgy cheeks.

"N... No." I twisted around, clutching Lilian and pulling us both backward. "The hotel... it's near the abbey ruins. We just want to find our way to the hotel!" The words spilled out in a desperate stream as I searched the horizon for an escape.

He pivoted towards his companions, his face hardening with grim determination. "Abbey ruins? Behold, lads, they return to lay siege to our abbey once more." His voice boomed like thunder in the gathering storm of confrontation. The group's anger swelled, their shouts pounding like war drums. The obese man knelt, picked up a massive rock, and aimed its glinting tip at my heart.

"Begone, swine! Begone from this sacred ground! Begone from our abbey's hallowed halls!" His words rang out like a battle cry as he hurled the stone through the air, its trajectory heading straight for me. I raised my arms to shield my face, and the stone struck my forearm with a sickening thud. I stumbled backward, cradling my arm.

The group surged forward as they snatched up handfuls of stones. "LEAVE!" Their voices rose in a collective howl as they charged towards us, hurling their makeshift weapons, each rock raining down in a relentless barrage.

We ran for safety, our feet pounding against the earth as we plunged into the refuse of the nearby woodland. The thick foliage clawed at us like deranged fingers, the soil giving way beneath our terrified strides. But the barefoot men pursued us relentlessly, their agile forms gliding with ease over the treacherous terrain, closing the gap between us until their hot breath was on our necks. Amidst the haunting echoes of Lilian's hysterical sobs and my own rattled breaths, the mossy underlayer of ground gave way to a dizzying drop. Without warning, we hurtled down a vertical slope. Our limbs thrashed, desperate to find a foothold on the sheer cliff face as our bodies tumbled downward in a gust of wind. We crashed onto the muck below with a thud, the impact sending shockwaves through our bones. The fall left us breathless and cloaked in gooey, clinging mud that coated us from head to toe like a second skin.

"You ok?" I asked Lilian between gasps.

"Honestly, I've been better," she replied, rising to her feet and looking back towards the cliff. "It's a miracle we weren't killed, that's quite the fall."

I rose and stood beside her.

Above us, the men skidded to a halt, hovering like ominous silhouettes against the skyline, still hurling rocks and curses down at us from their perch.

"What the hell is their problem?" I exclaimed, shooting a quick glance at Lilian. Her cheeks were flushed with exertion and dread, her slender frame quaking from chill and terror.

"I... I... I don't... know..." she stammered, her teeth chattering. "But I think it's best if we keep moving before they find a way down here."

We exchanged a determined nod, turned our backs on the men, and waded into a nearby river—the only way out of this hellhole. Our bodies sliced through the rushing currents until we emerged on the opposite shore.

As we dragged ourselves from the waters, I turned back toward the river and the cliff beyond. The men were still there, but their focus had shifted. The stout man had lost his footing and was hanging with one foot dangling over the ledge. His friends pulled on his arm as he clawed at the earth, his heels sending debris tumbling below as he struggled to regain his footing.

"Serves you right," I mumbled, a twinge of satisfaction pulsating through me. But then I saw a sight that swallowed my words. I staggered backward, my heel catching on a water-worn log lying on the beach. With a resounding thwack, I crashed onto my back, the impact jolting through me like a shockwave, knocking my lungs empty.

Lilian hurried back to my side and extended a hand, helping me into a seated position.

"Are you alright?" she asked, her voice laced with concern.

I shook my head, gasping, the searing burn refusing to subside. I was far from alright.

"What's hurting?" she asked, placing a hand on my back.

I shook my head again and raised a quavering finger, pointing back in the direction we had come. Her eyes followed. Her hand dropped from my back as she took two steps forward, her mouth hanging open as if her jaw had unhinged. Across the river, beyond the men on the hill, bathed in a pink hue, Dryburgh Abbey stood proudly against the skyline. Though weathered and worn by time, it was no longer ruined. Its spires soared toward the heavens, rising in improbable glory.

Chapter Eight

Tucked away in a secluded cave, sheltered under a canopy of twisted branches and spongy moss, we sought solace from the torrential storm outside. With our knees pulled tight to our chests, we huddled back-to-back, our shared exhaustion circulating between us. For hours we had bulldozed through the forest, driven by the determination to put as much distance between us and our attackers as possible.

We moved until exhaustion and the relentless downpour forced us to stop. Lilian spotted the lair first, a crevice splintered between two large rocks.

"We should see what is in there," she said as she dropped to her knees and crawled. I followed, allowing the gravity of our harrowing journey to settle over us like a suffocating shroud.

The fabric of our reality had frayed at the edges. We were adrift in a sea of unanswered questions.

Who were those men?

Why did they attack us?

Why did we share the same hallucination of a restored abbey?

The absence of explanation was a bitter pill to swallow for two seasoned researchers accustomed to unraveling mysteries and seeking answers. Amidst the swirling fog of our befuddlement, one thing remained clear: we were both geographically and existentially lost. The path before us was uncertain, with no beacon to light our way. In that chilling moment, our vulnerability settled over us, leaving us with nothing but the anguish of the unknown.

Lilian's teeth chattered as she squeezed into a smaller ball, coiling around herself to escape the chill that gnawed at her bones.

"You're freezing," I said.

"I'm...fi...fi...fine," she said, her words sluggish.

"You're not," I replied, worry forming crinkles on my forehead.

I scanned the floor of our makeshift housing for dry kindling until I found two sticks.

"Th… that… wo… won't… wor… work."

"Well, I have to try!" I snapped, my voice sharper than I intended. A fleeting wisp of hurt flickered in her eyes before giving way to a lingering look of exasperation.

Exhaustion weighed heavy on my limbs, every muscle protesting with soreness. My nerves had frayed like old rope. Our garments were saturated, clinging to our skin, and I knew the encroaching nightfall would bring a drastic drop in temperature. As the sun dipped below the horizon, our hideout turned colder, and the risk of illness grew greater. I lowered myself to the ground, placing my elbows as anchors in the soil. I gripped a stick in each hand, rubbing them together in a rhythmic motion.

Beside me, Lilian collapsed onto her side. "My fingers are tingling."

"I know," I said. "Just hold tight. I'm going to get this going."

For an hour I worked without rest, my hands moving in repetition until my wrists throbbed and my skin was imbedded with tiny pebbles. Lilian observed, her eyes childlike with fright, before she succumbed to exhaustion, her frame twitching in fitful slumber. The soft cadence of her snores punctuated the stillness, interrupted only by the occasional shivers that wracked her body with cold.

"Ten more minutes," I said to myself as I looked to her shivering frame, feeling helpless. "Ten more minutes, then you can give up." Ignoring the protest from my aching limbs I pressed on, the sticks beginning to fracture under the pressure of my grip. "Come on!" I cursed. At last, a tiny wisp of smoke curled upwards, the little coils swelling into a billowing cloud. Then, in a mesmerizing moment, a minute orange light flickered to life before my eyes.

"Oh my god! Yes!" I trumpeted, pumping my fists upward. I rose to my knees and scanned the nearby ground, grasping for any dry fuel to add to my fire. I turned to Lilian, ready to wake her and share the joy of my accomplishment. But as I pivoted back to my fledgling campfire, a gust of wind tore through the small cave, extinguishing the fragile flame. "Noooo!" A bestial yowl ripped from the innermost reaches of my soul. Blinding, red-hot rage surged through me like molten lava. With a furious kick, I sent the pile of twigs flying. Then I turned my fury to the den's roof, pounding it with my fists until blood trickled down my knuckles. The storm of anger subsided as I collapsed onto the damp earth. I shook with grievous sobs, covering my mouth to muffle the sounds. Even with the intensity of my outburst, Lilian remained undisturbed, a serene island amidst the crashing sea of my turmoil.

When the wracking cries finally stopped, I wiped my face with my shirt sleeve, the fabric now saturated with salty tears and mucus. I looked to Lilian, her small form still shivering, and crawled toward her. I studied her face; the rhythmic cadence of her snores had ceased, replaced by the sound of her breath escaping in fitful gasps. I leaned closer to examine her face in the muted light. Her eyes fluttered at the dreams behind them and her skin had grown pale. A watery trail of moisture glistened on her pointed nose and her thin lips, aquiver from the cold, were tinged with a sickly shade of purple.

Early-onset hypothermia, I thought, suppressing the surge of panic coursing through me. I inched toward her, wedging myself between her slender frame and the dank, earthen wall. With careful tenderness, I enveloped her in a bear hug. She hated physical contact, but in the face of our dire circumstances, I reasoned that our proximity was essential—our shared body heat a meager defense against the encroaching chill that threatened our survival. Lilian emitted a dovish sigh as she relaxed into me, settling into the sudden warmth. As I nestled into her, nuzzling my face into the nape of her neck, peace washed over me. If our fates were to succumb to the merciless elements, we would at least do so together.

Chapter Nine

In the depths of my dreams, the air was filled with the comforting aroma of root vegetables and cloves, wrapping around me like a warm veil. My stomach growled like a caged beast, a persistent reminder of how long it had been since our last meal. I knew I was dreaming, but I found solace in my brain's ability to offer me a moment of olfactory relief from the hunger that would plague me upon waking. A soft smile graced my lips as I basked in the illusion of the scent.

My hand still rested on Lilian's waist, where I had placed it the night before. She was no longer clammy to the touch and her steady breathing reassured me that she was alright. Our makeshift shelter had warmed through the night, cocooning us from the raging storm outside. My clothes, now dry, had peeled away from my skin, filling me with a comforting sense of normalcy amidst the chaos.

Lilian stirred, then rolled over and nestled her face against my chest. Her motion pulled me from my slumber, but I kept my eyes closed. For the second time in as many days, Lilian showed a tenderness unusual for her, and I wanted to savor it. Her hands curled around my abdomen, then trailed along my back, drawing me into an intimate embrace. A whirlwind of excitement surged, sending a fluttering sensation through my gut. Despite my efforts, a satisfied sigh escaped my lips as I settled into her hug. The pretense of unconsciousness was gone.

Lilian's finger tapped my back—once, twice, thrice. I shimmied to brush it off, but the taps continued, each one more insistent than the last. Cracking open one eye, I peered down at her. Her sweeping eyes locked onto mine as she mouthed her words. "There's someone here."

Bewilderment etched lines across my forehead as I gazed downward at Lilian and exaggeratedly whispered, "What?" Her nose scrunched with mounting frustration as she gestured behind her. I turned in the direction of her exaggerated nod. I hadn't been dreaming. The pungent perfume of cabbage and cloves flooded the small space, wafting from a cast-iron kettle hanging over a roaring flame.

A silver-haired woman stirred the concoction. Her back was to us, kneeling in the dirt at the den's entrance. The only distinguishing feature was the blackened soles of her bare feet, calloused and caked in soil. The last remnants of drowsiness fled from my body as my senses sharpened. I looked back at Lilian—her grimace mirrored my own.

My lips parted, poised to unleash a thunderous "Who the hell are you?" but I was interrupted.

"Ah, it is lovely to see you awake; ya gave me quite a scare." The voice was soothing and sweet, with only a hint of accent. It was as comforting as hot tea with honey. The silver-haired woman had turned to face us, balancing two hand-carved bowls of fragrant, bubbling broth on her palms.

Tall and slender, she moved with the fluid grace of a swan. The serene depths of her cerulean eyes shone with compassion, and her pearly, symmetrical smile seemed almost surgically enhanced. By all definitions, she was outstandingly attractive. We disentangled ourselves, shifting to sit with our backs against the cave's pitted wall.

The stranger, sensing our apprehension, wavered in her approach, her arms outstretched, a gesture more suited to calming a frightened animal than to calming humans.

"What we have here is pottage," she explained, her voice a gentle lullaby of reassurance. "It's pleasant and hearty, superb for warming you after a cold, miserable night."

She crouched, placed the soupy mixture within our reach, and then retreated slowly. She lowered herself to the ground and folded her spindly legs under her.

"It's delicious, I promise," she smiled as she gestured for us to eat.

Lilian and I exchanged anxious glances; even if this stranger had ill intentions, the allure of filling our empty stomachs was too persuasive to resist.

I cupped the bowl and brought it to my mouth. The herbaceous and briny amber broth glided down my throat, soothing my hunger and infusing my body with a pleasant euphoria. Once the liquid was gone, I skimmed my fingers over the dish's interior, picking up slivers of onion and cabbage and licking them clean.

"I'm so pleased you enjoyed it," she cooed, resting her chin in her hands.

"Thank you," I huffed, wiping my lips with the back of my hand.

"You are very welcome, my friends." She rose, picked up my empty bowl and glided back to the fire.

"Who are you?" Lilian questioned, dropping her dish in front of her with a hollow clang. I shot her a look. It's rare for me to show frustration at Lilian's perceived impoliteness, but given this stranger's compassion, I wished she had shown more gratitude. Lilian's shoulders drooped as if she had read my mind, and shame washed over me for ever wanting to alter anything about her unique personality.

The woman snatched Lilian's bowl too, unfazed by her curtness.

"Gelis," she curtsied, "Gelis Grey. I live nearby." She turned and poked the embers of her fire with a charred stick. "Last night, while I was out foraging, a sudden rainstorm drove me to seek asylum here. I was quite startled when I stumbled upon the two of you huddled together." A luxurious chuckle escaped her lips, a rich and velvety sound that lingered in the air. "I set up camp and prepared some hot food when I realized you two poor lambs were convulsing with cold."

I bowed my head, a quiet gesture of thanks. "We had a... very bad day yesterday and the kindness is much appreciated."

"It appears that you did," Gelis said, her eyes squinting. She paused and scratched her head before extending her pointer finger and swiveling it between Lilian and me. "Where did you get those funny garments?" she blurted.

"I believe it was Primark," I answered, tugging at the fabric of my oversized shirt. "It's a bit dated, but it's comfortable." Gelis's expression was a locked vault. She gazed past me, as if my words were spoken in a language she couldn't comprehend.

"There's one in Galashiels," I clarified.

Gelis tilted her head to the side, mimicking a playful puppy.

"I do not know a Primark from Galashiels," she responded. "Does he own a shop?"

Her reply prompted me to chortle.

"He owns MANY shops—all over the UK, giant department stores. You MUST have been to Primark," I wheezed between spurts of laughter.

Gelis puckered her lips thoughtfully before lifting her shoulders in a casual shrug. "Forgive me. I do not know of Mr. Primark."

I stopped laughing, scanning Gelis's face like a detective hunting for clues of sarcasm. She stared back at me, her expression vacant.

Lilian's eyes widened as she slowly turned her head from side to side, a look of incredulity eating away at her face.

"You two are odd," Gelis remarked. "But lucky for you, I appreciate odd!"

I bristled. "We are not odd! Yesterday, we woke up in a bloody field and then were assaulted by Robin Hood and his Merry Men when we asked for directions to the Dryburgh Abbey Hotel." The words spilled out of me, unrestrained by any concern for how "odd" I might seem. "They accused us of being here to attack the abbey," I scoffed, my fists clenching. "But we couldn't..."

"My precious angels," Gelis interjected, her subtle accent rolling through the air like a melody. "I mean no disrespect, but you must understand, more than once, the English laid siege to this land. The wounds are still fresh, and it is rare to see your kind here. I pass no judgment, I'm a bit of a traveller myself. Tend not to linger in one place too awful long. But I do ask that you consider the shock those men had when they saw you—their experiences with the English have been anything but amicable."

"I think 423 years is plenty of time to have healed from that wound!" I spat.

Gelis's face turned ghostly grey. She clutched her heart, swaying on her heels as if the ground beneath her was shifting.

"Gelis, I apologize. What an ass I am for saying that. That was out of line."

Gelis threw up her hand, a clear gesture of "Enough!" Her bright demeanor darkened, and she retreated to the farthest corner of the den, her fingers trailing along the wall as if seeking a hidden exit.

Lilian, who had been so subdued I nearly forgot she was there, reached out, her arms extending in a clumsy attempt at comfort. Gelis winced, her face tightening, begging Lilian to stay back.

An uneasy silence enveloped us.

"Who are you?" Gelis demanded, her voice sharp and edged with aggression as she mustered her courage and stepped closer.

"Lilian and Edgar," Lilian answered quickly.

"Where are you from?" Gelis's eyes narrowed, her face twisted in confusion.

"We are from Oxford University. We are here doing research, and I am sorry for upsetting you," I blurted out, lifting my hands in a gesture of surrender.

Gelis advanced on me, her steps jerky and agitated. She leaned in so close her breath warmed my face. She was tall, her eyes level with mine, and her stare pierced through me, making my pulse race.

"Women don't study at Oxford," she said, "so tell me the truth. I am here and I helped you, I at least deserve that."

Lilian now advanced, her shoulders squared as she faced off against Gelis.

"Ma'am, I am one of the most published historians in Oxford's storied history. I don't know what archaic ideas you hold but women have had a presence at Oxford since 1878 and..."

"What did you say?" Gelis interjected.

"I said, women have had a presence at Oxford since 1878," Lilian challenged.

Gelis growled, her teeth clenched. "What year do you think it is?"

I scoffed and moved away. "This is ridiculous, Gelis..."

Her hand shot out, her fingers pressing into my collarbone with surprising strength, pinning me in place.

"I asked what year you think it is?"

Her hold tightened, piercing pain shooting through my neck.

"2019!" I shouted, cowering behind my hands. Her grip slackened and her mouth fell open.

"Extraordinary," she whispered, her eyes darting between us.

She flitted around us, her lips moving in a constant murmur. She touched our attire, examining the textures between her fingers, her eyes studying the details and weaves with curiosity.

Lilian squirmed, pulling away from the intrusive touch.

"What is wrong with you?" she snapped, her body trembling with agitation.

Gelis spun to face us, twitching with giddy excitement.

"1596!" she shouted, throwing her arms in the air, her eyes rounded in solitary celebration.

Our lack of enthusiasm deflated her, and her features fell back to neutral.

"It is not the year 2019... my friends... This very moment... right this minute... the year is 1596."

Chapter Ten

We sat in stunned silence, our minds racing to grasp the incomprehensible reality that we were 423 years outside our own timeline.

Gelis fluttered around the room like a fledgling bird, her arms flapping as she tried to find balance. "In all my years, I've never seen something like this," she exclaimed.

Despite every instinct urging us to flee, we stayed rooted to our seats, paralyzed by the bizarre circumstances.

"What should we do?" Gelis tapped a finger on her chin. "I know! Let's get you out of these strange clothes and into something more fitting. Yes, that will be our first step. Alright! Both of you, up now!" Gelis's voice cut through the haze in my mind as she seized Lilian's wrist with a blistering grasp and pulled her to her feet. The impact caught Lilian off guard, and she stumbled before regaining her balance.

Gelis reached for me, but I jerked my arm away, glaring at her. I had no idea what game this woman was playing, but I wanted no part of it.

"Okay" she said, raising her palms in a gesture of defense. "Edgar, I'm sorry, but we can't stay here. These woods are a common passageway for travelers, and if we want to avoid drawing attention, we need to blend in. You can't look like you've just stepped out of another century." I crossed my arms, trying to muster some defiance, and looked to Lilian for reassurance. She met my gaze and shrugged.

"Don't know what other option we have, Ed, neither of us know how to get back to the hotel from here," she huffed.

With one last glare at Gelis, I rose and wiped the damp earth from my pants. The confusion of our surroundings and the unsettling reality of our situation pressed in on me. Despite everything, it was clear that our best chance at getting out of this godforsaken cave lay in following Gelis.

"Good. Now let's go!" Gelis lifted the cast iron pot from its hook above the smoldering campfire, the coals now a bed of glowing embers. With practiced ease, she placed it in a large burlap sack and slung it over her shoulder. A slight hop secured the load, and she flashed us a quick smile as she stepped through the makeshift doorway. Lilian and I exchanged uncertain glances then trailed off behind her, keeping a cautious distance as we ventured into the unknown.

Gelis's feet glided across the woodland carpet, immune to the twigs and roots in her path. She moved with unbridled freedom, unfazed by the crunching sticks or the squelching soil between her toes. Ahead of us, she darted through the underbrush while Lilian and I struggled to keep up. We stumbled over fallen branches, slipping on the muddy ground, lagging further back. She hummed a tune as she walked, her head turning regularly to check that we were still in sight.

I trotted along in silence, inspecting the tree line and footpath for any landmark that might jog my memory. Nothing. In the daylight, the forest was an entirely different place. My sense of direction had evaporated, leaving me disoriented amidst the altered landscape.

"Is she crazy, or are we?" Lilian's voice trembled, each word dripping with the fear of either answer.

"She is," I responded, still watching for any hint of familiarity. "But I think she's harmless crazy, and right now, we are lost.

Ignore the time travel stuff, let's just get her to lead us back to civilization and then we can ditch her."

Lilian grabbed my arm to draw my eyes from my surroundings. "But what if she's not wrong, Edgar?" Her pupils dilated, pleading for understanding. "You were there—you saw Lizzy's face; you felt the darkness." Anxiety twisted her usual composed tone into a frantic, high-pitched squeak.

"Alright, alright," I chuckled, "maybe she's not the crazy one... maybe it's you!" I nudged her and gave a playful wink.

Her jaw clenched, and an angry vein pulsed at her temple as she marched off, closing the gap between her and Gelis.

"I was joking!" I shouted, my words bouncing off her back as she retreated, oblivious to my attempt at humor.

We trudged along in single file, leaves and twigs crunching underfoot. I abandoned any hope of orientation, and instead turned my mind to crafting witty retorts for Lilian, ready to strike if she reignited our argument.

"Here we are my friends!" Gelis's voice rang out from ahead, snapping me out of my anger-fueled daydream. Realizing the growing distance, I hurried toward her, the thought of being left alone in this unfamiliar place propelling me forward.

Gelis stood at the threshold of an old wooden cottage nestled in a secluded alcove. Gnarled rose bushes curled around the building, their thorns piercing through neon-green moss that fought to consume any exposed wood. The chimney, crumbled at the top, emitted a faint plume of smoke. Her eyes sparkled. "It's not much, but it's home... and I built it myself, which I consider quite the accomplishment."

She threw her entire body into pushing the door open. It swayed unsteadily on its rusty hinges, groaning in protest. As a small crack appeared, a fat orange tabby darted forward, greeting Gelis with excited mews. The cat weaved between her ankles, its long, striped tail wrapping around her shin.

"I know, my friend; I am so sorry for being late," Gelis cooed, moving to a spacious counter at the far end of the room, unclogging the doorway for us. Still stewing from our earlier disagreement, Lilian shuffled inside without a second thought and slumped against the wall, her arms intertwined in a pronounced pout. I hesitated at the threshold, still uneasy with Gelis's fantastical claims of time travel, and surveyed the area before stepping in myself.

The home was one room. Blankets nestled in a corner hinted at a makeshift bedroom, while a small wooden table opposite the bed served as a dining area. The epicenter of the space was the kitchen, which dominated much of the floor plan, snaking around in an L-shape at the front of the house. Above me, the roof was adorned with bundles of herbs, each vibrant color at a varying stage of the drying process. A spicy, inviting aroma wafted through the air, masking the faint smell of dampness that clung to the poorly insulated structure. A large, imposing stone fireplace stood to my right, its interior blackened from years of roaring fires. There were no TVs or overhead lights, just pillared candles resting on most available surfaces of the space.

Gelis moved about the kitchen and pulled a clay pot from a bottom cupboard. She poured its contents, a thick and yellow-hued milk, into a dish. The orange tabby trotted over and lapped from the dish as Gelis wiped her hands on her smock and gave the tomcat an affectionate pat on the head.

My face scrunched. *Seems unsanitary*, I thought.

"This is Horis," she said. "He showed up here a few years ago, and I thought he would be useful in keeping down the pests. Turns out he's developed a liking for lounging and milk that has outweighed his natural instincts to mouse."

A small smile tugged at the corners of my mouth as the well-loved tabby purred and pranced with excitement, milk beading on his whiskers. Glancing at Lilian, I saw a mirrored twinkle in her eyes, our earlier anger melted away, replaced by dimpled grins as the cat wove its way into our hearts.

Now more at ease, Lilian moved about the room. She examined the fireplace, then looked up at the ceiling, searching for signs of plumbing or indoor electricity—anything that might hint at modernity, but found nothing.

Gelis's eyes followed Lilian's every move as she surveyed her home. Instead of continuing her claims of time travel, she offered a knowing look before gliding toward the bedside. She knelt and pulled back layers of weighty blankets to reveal an elaborately carved chest. Thick leather straps secured the trunk, and it took significant persistence and unexpected strength to wrestle the bindings loose. A treasure trove of luxurious fabrics spilled forth as she lifted the lid.

"We must get you out of those clothes," Gelis declared as she rolled the cloth into a giant mass. "Something in here should work." She carried the heap over to us, spreading the garments across the expansive kitchen countertops.

She handed me a pair of scratchy grey trousers and a beige flowing shirt. Then, she hesitated, her fingers lingering on the fabric of a dress. The gown was a masterpiece: soft pink and silky with a wide skirt and delicate white flowers that crept from the waistline downward in spiraling clusters. Gelis released an audible breath, her eyes glazing over with memories before handing the dress to Lilian.

"Where did you find this?" Lilian murmured, her mouth agape as she eyed Gelis's worn linen smock noting every crease and fray.

"Just some... old... heirlooms," Gelis hummed, her voice distant. "I'm not a young lady anymore, and the dress is meant for young ladies." Her lips formed a strained smile. "It will look beautiful and fitting on you!" She patted Lilian on the arm then turned away, giving us as much privacy as the cramped quarters of her home would allow.

I peeled off my soiled clothing, brushing off the grime that clung to my skin, and crumpled them into a heap. While I didn't believe Gelis's talk of time travel, the sheer relief of slipping into a new outfit was undeniable. Even if this was some elaborate prank, the wish to be dry and somewhat clean outweighed any worry of humiliation.

The trousers chafed against me, hanging heavily from my hips and held up by a makeshift belt of coarse rope. The shirt draped loosely over my torso, the front cut into a deep vee. As I fumbled to adjust the ill-fitting garment, I turned to face Lilian.

She stood in the corner, arms wrapped around herself, clutching her new outfit to her. Her eyes flickered with nervous uncertainty, darting about the room. Noticing her discomfort, I gestured for her to come closer. "Need some help?" I offered.

She nodded and shuffled toward me, her movements awkward and unsure. She swiveled her back to me, revealing snow-white, impossibly soft skin untouched by sunlight. My hands trembled as I picked up the two silk strings at the bottom of her exposed back. I began threading the delicate strands through the eyelets, creating each small X with care. As I pulled the bodice tight, Lilian's breath hitched and her petite frame transformed before me, the fabric drawing in at her waist and accentuating her hourglass figure. The air crackled with tension, every unintentional brush against her sending jolts of awareness through me. She shivered slightly, and I wasn't sure if it was from the cold or something else. I tied a stunted bow at the top of the corset, where it nestled snug at the junction of her spine and the base of her skull, and let my hand linger for a moment.

"There you go," I said, shaking my thoughts from my head and giving her a friendly pat on the shoulder.

Lilian turned to face me; her arms extended like wings. "Well," she said as she gave a small twirl, her eyes sparkling with a blend of embarrassment and amusement. "How do I look?"

She was a vision. The creamy hues of her attire accentuated her milky skin and deep brown eyes, drawing me in with their depth. Her hair, often unremarkable, now shimmered with dazzling highlights of amber that flitted in the light, and the shape of her, so often hidden behind those pantsuits, would be the envy of any woman.

"Pe-perfect," I stammered, my cheeks flushing a brilliant red.

She shuffled. "You look wonderful, too," she said as her fingers nervously smoothed the skirt.

Gelis approached and pushed our shoulders together. "Ravishing," she gushed, admiring her work. "It's as if they were made for you."

Chapter Eleven

The days after our arrival at Gelis's cottage flowed with a gentle, comforting rhythm. The cottage and its surrounding gardens were timeless and tranquil and enveloped us in its soothing clasp. Each morning began with the rustling of leaves in the breeze and the gradual warming of sunlight filling the one-room abode. We found joy in simple routines—cooking hearty meals over a crackling fire and reading by the soft glow of candlelight. These small, intimate moments brought a peace that modern life had buried away within us. Though our beds were little more than rough pallets, we slept soundly each night, wrapped in heavy homemade blankets that pressed against our weary bodies. The glow of the dying embers and the exhaustion from a day's labor lulled us into deep, dreamless sleep.

Well, almost dreamless. Every evening since we arrived, the recollection of tying Lilian's dress replayed in an endless loop.

Her delicate skin, the way the fabric hugged her contours and the subtle scent of her hair lingered in my thoughts. My fingers twitched recalling the smooth silk strings, my body tingled at the memory of her warmth. My heart ached as I came to terms with the truth: I again, was seeing her as more than a friend. I had been down this road before in France, and promised myself to not do it again. Our friendship was precious to me, but now, in the quiet of the night, I couldn't deny the growing desire I felt for her. It was a forceful, unexpected feeling, and I feared it would change everything.

While I enwrapped myself in the enchantment of our surroundings and my secret fantasies, Lilian remained steadfast in her quest for answers. Like a determined sleuth, she shadowed Gelis, peppering her with inquiries and theories about her wild allegations of time travel.

Initially, Gelis met Lilian's questions with patience, sharing her insights and encouraging her questions with thoughtful nods. But as days extended into a week and Lilian's persistence showed no signs of waning, Gelis's initial enthusiasm began to decline. Her eager responses dwindled to wordless grunts, and she started finding excuses to distance herself from Lilian.

"Gelis is avoiding me," Lilian said to me one evening in the garden. "I think I've annoyed her." She gave a backyard hen a gentle push and tucked its egg into a wicker basket. Gelis had left early in the morning to forage and hadn't yet returned. I imagine it was a guise to have a day away from Lilian's persistent interrogations.

"Well, you have been pretty relentless with the questioning," I said, lobbing a second egg into the basket.

"It's what I do." Lilian shrugged and then turned her back to me. "You know Ed, I've been searching this place for any sign of modernity for a week now and there's nothing. Everything Gelis does, the way she speaks, it is all in line with her theory about time travel."

I shot a skeptical leer in her direction.

"Don't look at me like that," she huffed. "It's a harsh realization for me as well, but I cannot come up with any other explanation for our situation. I know you see this as some whimsical medieval holiday experience, but I'm starting to think this isn't just the way *she* lives. It's the way everyone lives, and we are the ones out of place. I would like to find a town and confirm my suspicions, and maybe see if we can find Lizzy. If we are here, I imagine she is too."

I sighed. While I yearned to remain in the tranquil garden, with Horis purring at my side and my daydreams of Lilian for company, the time had come to face our reality—not only for Lilian's sake, but also to protect Gelis's fragile peace of mind.

"Ok Lilian, I think it's insane, but maybe you are right, we can't stay here forever."

On our eighth evening with our friend, as twilight draped the cottage in the dreamy hues of dying daylight, and Gelis finally returned empty handed from her foraging trip, I mustered the nerve to break the enchantment of this place. I placed two bowls of steaming soup before them and uttered the words I dreaded to say out loud.

"We are so grateful for your hospitality, Gelis, but I think it's time for Lilian and me to find our way back to... wherever we go from here."

Lilian's eyes sparkled with excitement, while Gelis's shone with relief.

"I'm sorry I waited so long," I said, "I just don't know where to begin. Your suggestion that we moved through time is hard to believe, but we can't stay here forever. I think it's time I admit that whatever is happening is beyond reason, and we should take steps to right what has happened."

Lilian's head swiveled between Gelis and me, anticipation flushing the bridge of her nose. *God she is beautiful*, I thought.

"We may have a solution," Lilian blurted out, bringing me back to reality. "Or at least a viable starting point."

She nodded toward Gelis and gestured for her to speak.

"Not far from here is a village," Gelis began, her voice carrying a note of caution. "It's not the friendliest of places. They have endured some... unusual circumstances in recent years." Her jaw clenched as she contemplated continuing. "But there's a young woman there, a healer and midwife. She might be open to hearing your story. However, the community isn't kind to outsiders, especially English ones. Before we go, you should work on your accents and create a more believable backstory than traveling 423 years through time."

A wry smile curved Gelis's lips, and as if on cue, the absurdity of our predicament struck us all at once. Laughter erupted, bubbling up and filling the room with its infectious joy. We huddled around the fire's glow, the flickering flames painting playful shadows on our cheeks, and began crafting a plan.

The following two days became a crash course in dialect and character study. With determined focus, we practiced our accents until they flowed with ease. Every task we undertook became a lesson in the ways of the present word. The way we walked, and talked and worked all tweaked to mask our modern-day mentalities.

We crafted a believable narrative, choosing to keep our names to minimize the possibility of mistakes. We decided that Lilian and I were to play siblings from the borderlands whose parents, driven by desperation, sent us away after brutal English conflicts ravaged our homeland.

On the evening before our departure we gathered in Gelis's kitchen, barefoot and joyous as she quizzed us on the details of our new lives, her interrogation juxtaposed with the aroma of baking bread she had placed over the open hearth.

As the sun dipped below the horizon, a golden glow gleamed through the small windows, and Gelis sighed with contentment, her eyes reflecting the warmth of the dying light. She stretched her hands to her lower back and pushed, easing the stiffness from hours spent in the hard-backed wooden chairs.

"Well, my friends, it appears you've got a good handle on it. Shall we rest while we can? Tomorrow's journey will be a tiring one."

We exchanged shrewd glances, our heads dipping in agreement, we said our goodnights and nestled into the snug embrace of our beds, their comfort wrapping around us one last time.

Chapter Twelve

Underneath the weighty blanket, my legs twitched involuntarily, my mind whirring like an overworked engine. I turned onto one side, then onto my back, then onto my other side. Each position invited a new and more invasive thought. Morning blossomed before sleep found me. The sun peeking over the horizon painted the inside of my eyelids and I groaned.

Horis, who quickly grew accustomed to my willingness to cuddle, was nestled into the crook between my knees. His gentle purrs sent soothing vibrations through me.

I rolled over, pulled him into my arms and wrapped him in a loving hug, pressing my nose into his warm fur. The scent was like the memory of summer mornings, a mixture of dewy grass and soil. Tears welled up in my eyes.

Today was the last day I would see him. It might be the last day I see Gelis too. It was also the last day I would allow myself to ruminate on the moment I shared with Lilian, shutting the door on the possibility of anything more than friendship.

I had come to that decision during my sleepless night.

Since the dress incident—as I now referred to it in the private confides of my mind—every glance at her stirred up a cocktail of longing. I found myself avoiding her eyes and biting my lip to keep from saying too much. Lilian trusted me, and revealing my feelings could disrupt the delicate balance of our friendship—or worse, cause her discomfort. All night, my mind flipped between thoughts of Lilian and Gelis. Leaving this place meant abandoning Horis and Gelis to my memories. When we returned to our own time, however and whenever that happened, the world housing my companions—this untamed woman and her plump little cat—would vanish from reality. Their existence would be forgotten in the annals of time. My grief was twofold: the end of something that could not be, and the inevitable loss of my friends.

Part of me longed to stay, to spend my days in this little oasis. But by the time I rolled myself over in bed, Lilian was already at the door, her dress half-laced, the rhythmic tapping of her foot amplifying through the quiet room. She was ready to go.

I sat up and stretched unhurriedly, then picked up my clothes with quiet contemplation.

"Ready," I said as I tied the lace of my boot into a neat little bow, pushing the thought of lacing Lilian's dress out of my mind for the final time.

"About time," Lilian huffed. "Let's go." She stomped out the door without a second glance.

"Bye little buddy," I cooed to Horis, planting a slopping kiss on his forehead, "you be a good boy, alright?" He let out a playful *meep* and batted at my shoelace as if to say "*not a chance.*" I cast one final longing look at the cottage, then crossed through the doorway and into the unknown.

As we headed toward town, I trailed behind Gelis and Lilian, my steps slow and reluctant.

The walk stretched on along a dense and unmarked route, which only exasperated my foul mood.

"How often do you travel this way?" I questioned, extracting a string of cobweb from my lips.

"It has been many years since I've visited this village," Gelis replied. "I used to come here often, but then the troubles came, and I felt it best to keep to myself."

"That's the second time you've mentioned that. What troubles?"

"You're snagged Lilian," Gelis said, changing the subject and kneeling to free the hem of Lilian's dress from a rogue branch. As she tugged, the fabric ripped with a harsh sound and Gelis's nostrils flared as she met Lilian's downward gaze.

"I've got it," Lilian said curtly as she snatched the dress from Gelis's hands and stormed off, her footsteps pounding against the ground.

"What's that about?" I asked, Lilian's sudden sour mood distracting me from the fact that Gelis still hadn't answered my question.

"Lord knows with that girl," Gelis replied. "You've got your hands full with that one lad." Gelis shook her head and followed Lilian down the path. "You're going the wrong way!" she shouted. "You insufferable twat."

I stopped in my tracks, shocked at first by Gelis's angry words, but as we continued to struggle through a thicket of thorny briars, I forgave her. This was an unpleasant journey, and tensions were high all around.

"Finally!" I muttered to myself as I fought off one final tangle of nettle and stumbled out onto a narrow arterial road.

Gelis and Lilian, relieved to be free of the barbs and pricks of the forest, had already made up and were again all smiles.

Our pace quickened as we passed over a small creek covered by a wooden bridge, where we were greeted by the faraway drones of civilization—the first buzz we had encountered in over a week.

Lilian and I stopped, the reality of the situation hitting us like a brick wall. We exchanged nervous glances as Gelis urged us forward.

"Not far now," she cooed. "Remember your story and stay close to me."

The scene before us unfolded like a painting from the Middle Ages. Thatched-roof buildings lined a dusty street, their timbers teetering in defiance of gravity. The air thrummed with the sounds of village life, and there were people everywhere. After the solitude of Gelis's home, this busy town center was an olfactory overload. The overwhelming sights and smells made me feel as if I were teetering on the hind legs of a chair. My head swiveled as I looked around to my right, where a dirty, toothless woman scolded a child and dragged him away by his arm, his bare toes grazing the dusty path. Ahead of me, a red-faced, pudgy man was swinging a large trout in the direction of another and yelling about the increased cost of fish. And everywhere around me the pungent aroma of damp fur, stale smoke, and human waste assaulted my nose. The scene was dizzying, but I still noticed there were no cars or electric lights, no billboards flashing overhead, nor the roar of jets shooting across the sky. Gelis was telling the truth.

I quickened my stride to keep pace with Gelis and Lilian, a sudden surge of self-consciousness washing over me. Even through the hubbub of the market square, the villagers had taken notice of us strangers and their gaze lingered on us like ghosts haunting every forward step.

"Ignore them," Gelis murmured from the corner of her mouth. But as we passed each shop and home, my courage shrank as mutters of disapproval trailed us loud enough to be heard despite their attempt at subtlety.

It took only a few minutes before we reached the end of the Main Street. The clamor of voices melted away into a far-off whirr, and my shoulders relaxed as the hustle and bustle gave way to rows of quaint houses set further apart and nestled amidst small pastures of livestock and gardens. A few stray chickens meandered across our path, their beady eyes focused on the ground as they pecked for scraps.

We walked in single file with Gelis leading the way. She took a sharp left, and Lilian and I nearly collided as we tried to make the unexpected turn. Gelis continued down a narrow lane until she came to a small gate. It rose only to hip level and swung gently in the breeze.

"Almost there now," she said as she pushed it open and continued forward.

I studied my surroundings with wonder, my anxieties melting away as the pathway erupted with the calming scent of lavender and chamomile. Enveloping us were sprawling gardens, bursting with untamed blooms that dotted the lush grass like dabs of paint on a palette. The path meandered past lilacs whose blooms were so prolific the branches bowed down and brushed our shoulders. I extended my hands and ran them over the tops of hollyhocks buzzing with bees. We crossed through an archway weaved with rhododendrons and finally emerged on the steps of a small stone house.

Gelis reached out and knocked three times. Inside, the soft patter of bare feet on hardwood drifted out through the open window beside us.

The door creaked open, revealing a large green eye framed by a curtain of dusty silver hair. Suddenly, the door swung wide and slammed against the exterior wall, making both Lilian and I jump.

In the doorway stood a petite woman, her round figure reminiscent of a teapot. Her face bore the telltale signs of youth—rosy cheeks and bright eyes—but the rest of her features were soft and marked age. She was clad in a simple grey frock with a plain white apron, and wrinkled skin peeked out at her collarbone and wrists.

With open arms, she embraced Gelis as if they were old friends.

"Iona!" Gelis exclaimed, returning the greeting with enthusiasm. "These are my friends, Edgar and Lilian."

Iona peeked at us over Gelis's shoulder. "Welcome, my friends. Come in." She released Gelis and gestured inside.

We both shifted on our feet, apprehensive to use our practiced accents in a real-life situation. Silently, we shuffled through the doorway into a spacious, open cottage. Like Gelis's home, it was adorned with bundles of herbs hanging from the beams, their earthy scents mingling in the air. Every surface was adorned with bouquets of fresh peonies, their blossoms open and inviting.

Iona peered out her window before snapping the flowery pink curtain shut. Lilian contemplated interjecting. "*That won't do much good considering there is no glass,*" I imagined her saying. She poised to speak but then hesitated, remembering she couldn't retort in her usual prim and proper English accent. She crossed her arms and looked down at her feet.

Iona flitted about her home, snatching up pillows in various shades of pink and arranging them in a cozy circle of chairs in her living area. With a sweeping gesture, she invited us to sit. We complied, sinking into the inviting cushions with relief after our long journey.

She plopped herself down across from us, her chair creaking disconcertingly under the stress of her roundness. I flinched, fearing the chair might break, but it held firm.

Lilian and I perched on our seats like scolded schoolchildren, shooting nervous glances across the room at the two older ladies engrossed in their animated gossip, who had seemingly forgotten we were there.

After what felt like an eternity, Iona turned to us with a radiant smile.

"I received correspondence from Gelis that I could be expecting visitors."

Iona blinked, the speed of her fluttering lashes causing Lilian to shift uncomfortably in her seat.

"Thank you for allowing us to come. We have a bit of a... delicate matter to discuss with you, Iona," Gelis said, wringing her hands in her lap. "I think you will understand the need for assurance that this conversation goes no further than this circle."

Iona gave a solemn nod.

I held my breath in anticipation as Gelis began to unravel the details of our expedition thus far.

"These two are not family as I noted in my letter," Gelis began, her voice tinged with guilt. "I apologize for the dishonesty, but I was afraid of it being intercepted. You know how nosy the villagers can be."

Iona scoffed, a playful glint in her eyes, and Gelis gave her a cheeky wink.

"I discovered these two huddled together by the abbey during last week's thunderstorm. They were dressed in queer garments, and when we got talking, they said they work... or worked," she corrected herself, causing Lilian to cringe at the use of the past tense, "at a university, studying Scotland and its history of witches. It gets stranger though, for you see, they appear to have moved through time."

Iona stiffened, her head swiveling around the room as if scanning for unseen listeners lurking in hidden corners.

"Whatever do you mean? There are no witches here," Iona quivered, more frightened by the word witch then the concept of time travel.

Lilian's tone turned steady and informative. "No, there are no witches here, but the Scottish people believed there to be plenty. After King James published his book *Demonology*, accusations spread like wildfire. Women and men across Scotland were tortured and murdered in the thousands, accused of witchcraft."

Lilian's matter-of-fact statement hit Gelis and Iona like a slap. Iona's eyes bulged and the color drained from her face.

"King James's book? I know nothing of it... and tortured how?" Iona stammered.

Lilian's excitement swelled as she delved into her life's work. "He published it in 1597. It is essentially a dissertation on devil worship, witchcraft, and demons in Scotland and how society can fight against it. As for the torture... there were many horrible methods. Some had their fingernails torn out, others were pricked with razor-sharp iron needles, looking for a spot on the body that felt no pain. Some were placed in spiked barrels and rolled down hills to see if they would survive..." Lilian's voice trailed off as she became suddenly aware of Iona's discomfort.

"When?" Iona asked, her chin quivering.

"Excuse me?" Lilian leaned in, turning her ear to Iona.

Iona cleared her throat, her voice shifting from a mere whisper to a muted murmur. "When did they torture people...?"

A stillness settled over the room. Lilian and I were accustomed to analyzing events from the comfortable distance of a few hundred years. It was easy to draw conclusions when the suffering was confined to the pages of history books. But now, sitting before us were women whose lived experiences made such atrocities harsh, unforgiving realities.

Lilian squirmed in her seat, her eyes darting about as she recalled Gelis's jubilant exclamation in the cave—1596. She procrastinated but ultimately sided with the truth. "It began in 1597," she answered. "You must have heard about the women killed a few years back, not far from here."

Gelis and Iona exchanged a knowing glance. Lilian, almost unable to control her insatiable need to share her knowledge, rambled on.

"King James claimed those women conjured storms to prevent him and his Danish bride from returning to Scotland. They confessed, but only because they were subjected to horrific torture." Lilian paused for dramatic effect, a terrible decision from my vantage point. "Two hundred people died because of that one event. But it doesn't stop there. It happens again... some of the worst will happen soon, in mere months. This time, it will be more violent, more awful."

Gelis and Iona's muscles tensed, their breaths quickening, but Lilian did not relent.

"Over the next year, the situation will escalate. It will begin in Saint Andrews and spread throughout Scotland. Thousands will die, some will flee, and very few will be found innocent once accused." She turned to Gelis, locking eyes. "If you are correct and the current year is 1596, then women like you two, living in the woods, caring for women, will not fare well in the chaos coming. We need to find our way back to our own time and place, and you need to seek safety beyond these old woodlands—and soon."

I lifted my eyes from my lap, turning to face Gelis and Iona. A kaleidoscope of emotions played across their faces: terror, fiery rage, and finally disbelief.

Stillness descended once more, thick with discomfort, until Gelis's meek and unfamiliar whisper broke it. "If what you say is true, I will find a way to manage," she murmured.

"But it does not explain how you both ended up huddled in a cave in the middle of nowhere. How did you manage to move backward through time?" added Iona.

Lilian's frustration at the downplay of her warning was evident. Sensing the brewing storm, I stepped in, hoping to defuse the tension before it escalated into a full-blown argument.

"It's... hard to explain. I don't have much of an explanation at all, really—at least not one that makes any sense."

Iona looked from Lilian to me, her arms folding in defiance, challenging us to at least try.

"Lilian received correspondence that called us to the Borders. A woman claimed to have found a document that required Lilian's expertise. While Lilian was meeting with her, I was at the abbey and stumbled upon an old monument and a weathered old book."

Gelis and Iona sat transfixed, their mouths hanging open.

"When Lilian and I met up, she showed me what the source had—a page from a book, a page from the same book I had discovered."

"Ooooh," the women gasped in unison.

"I know! Remarkable, right?" Fueled by their intrigue, my storytelling became more animated. I stood with my hands above me, swinging my head in perverse circles as I recounted the bewildering incantation Lizzy had uttered at the Temple of the Muses, and I jumped about the room, dodging imaginary rocks when I regaled them with the harrowing escape from the men in the abbey. As I concluded the tale, I rested a hand on Lilian's shoulder, squeezing gently as I told them of my fear of losing her and huddling together to keep warm. Lilian looked up at me, her lips slightly parted, a softness stretching across her face. Our eye contact lingered, and the familiar stir of want awakened within me. I moved my hand, cleared my throat, and sat back in my chair. "It seems far-fetched, I know," I said, rubbing the nape of my neck.

"My goodness," Gelis said, her hand lingering over her heart. "I now understand why you were apprehensive when you woke to find me in your cave. I am sorry for the experience you have had."

Iona nodded along, her mouth pulled into a straight line of sympathy.

I tilted my head. "You believe me?"

"We have no reason not to believe you—and I certainly have no better explanation than the one you've given," Gelis exclaimed, propping her head on her chin. "Though... your tale makes me wonder if, perhaps, there is magic among us after all." She rose from her seat, leaving Lilian and me alone in the circle with Iona. Her words lingered, secreting a weighty shadow over the group. "Maybe there is magic among us after all."

The gravity of our situation began to settle over us as we sagged deep into our seats.

Academically, our tale defied reason. Logically, it was implausible. Yet, here we were, entangled in a narrative that was pulled from the very pages of a fairy tale and nobody seemed to be questioning it, which was counterintuitive to everything we had been taught as researchers. Whether it was legitimate sorcery, or something else, one thing was sure: this was beyond our comprehension. If Gelis was correct about the year, we were about to plunge into a perilous phase of human existence. We needed to find a way back to our former state of consciousness—or time—whatever the truth might be.

The room spun, and I gripped the edge of my chair to steady myself. Noticing my unsteadiness, Iona rose and shuffled into the kitchen. She retrieved a bundle of herbs from the drying rack above the front door and turned her back to us as she plucked the small yellow petals from the stalks, placing them into a hand-carved stone mortar and crushing them into a fine powder.

"This is all so far-fetched," Lilian exclaimed, leaping from her seat and following Iona across the floor to the kitchen.

Neither woman responded. They had disappeared inside themselves, wrapped in their worries, their faces a canvas of contemplation.

"It seems far-fetched to us, too," Lilian rambled, her words spilling out in a rush as she paced about the room. "But I need to ask you, do you know of an Isobel or Lizzy here or nearby? Could you help us sort out this..."

Lilian's hands traced small circles in the air searching for the right words. "...misunderstanding?" She cringed, knowing "misunderstanding" was a gross understatement of our situation.

Gelis trotted to where Iona stood and let out an airy chuckle. She began pulling clay mugs from a shelf, arranging them on the rustic table as if she were in the comfort of her own kitchen.

"My dear girl, I know not of an Isobel nor of a Lizzy—though I must admit, I do not often stray far from my home."

"I... " Iona chewed at the corner of her thumbnail and cast a quick look at Gelis. "I... I don't know either... but the book... tell me about the book."

"Oh, it was beautiful," Lilian proclaimed. "Tiny—it would fit in your pocket, with a lovely tan leather cover. The lettering on the front was engraved in elegant cursive gold letters: 'Seilbh Iseabail Alasdair,'" she said, her voice singing.

Iona nodded. "Do you have the book?"

I opened my mouth to explain the tussle again when Lilian cut me off. "It got lost in the scuffle."

Disappointment shadowed Iona's face. "Well, that is too bad. Our Angus always carried a small book, which was more of a diary, I think I would recognize it if I saw it." she said casually. She had finished crushing the flowers into a vibrant mustard dust and was now pouring steaming water from the kitchen hearth over them.

"Who is Angus?" I asked, moving from my seat in the living room to one at the table.

"She, like me, helps..." She paused and corrected herself. "Helped... mothers." Her back was still to us as she stirred the steaming mixture. "She lived around these parts until not long ago when a rich townswoman's birth went bad."

"What happened?" Lilian asked, joining me.

"She lost the wee lad—and the mother, too. The father was furious. He wanted blood, blamed her for their deaths, and made-up horrible stories about her. She fled during the night, which only fueled the rumors about her." Iona's spoon slipped from her grasp, clanging on the table as the grim reality of Lilian's warnings sank in. Her knuckles turned white as she steadied herself against the thought.

"Oh, Angus," she sniffled. "I've heard from the other women who help that she's out there—but I don't know where. Some say she went toward the Capital but that is as much I know. The man is still pursuing her determined to get vengeance." Her posture relaxed as she became bewitched by her memories. "Her beauty... oh, she was an outstanding beauty. Fire-red hair that curled in fashionable corkscrews and eyes so green they looked like gemstones."

Iona lumbered to the table and placed her concoction in the middle, the fragrant steam curling into the air. She returned to the kitchen and produced a large slab of meat, a wedge of sour-smelling cheese, and a crusty loaf of bread, which she arranged in front of Lilian and me.

"Please, eat," she said, dropping into her chair with a weary sigh and resting her chin on her palm.

She glanced toward the open window, where the curtain fluttered in the evening breeze, revealing the fading sunlight outside.

"I suggest you stay here tonight—it's too treacherous to travel," Iona advised, patting Lilian on the shoulder. "Tea?" she asked while already pouring small portions of the herbal mixture into each of our mugs.

"Please," Lilian said, tearing a piece of bread from the loaf and breaking off a small corner of the cheese. As she spoke, she absentmindedly tore the bread into smaller and smaller pieces. "The Capital... as in Edinburgh. How long is the journey from here?"

"About a day by foot if you travel by road, a day and a half if you choose to stick to the woods," said Gelis, rejoining the table and eyeing Lilian's methodical eating habits with intense curiosity. "Given your... circumstances, I suggest you do the latter."

"Well... right now, Angus is our only lead," Lilian said, her voice tinged with uncertainty. "I know the chances are slim that her diary is the same book that brought us here, but what other option do we have?" She searched my face for reassurance. "To Edinburgh?" she asked.

"I guess we have no other choice," I muttered. "To Edinburgh."

"To Edinburgh!" echoed Gelis, raising her glass of lukewarm tea in the air.

We raised ours too in a weary toast.

Iona leaned into me and patted my arm. "That will help with the nerves, dear."

"I need all the help I can get," I scoffed as I tipped my head back and downed the contents of the cup. The drink's tart and peaty flavor reminded me of my grandfather's evening whiskey and pipe, smoky and comforting.

We ate until our bellies were full and then retired to the living space, where one by one our eyelids grew heavy, and conversations faded into whispers. I watched Lilian, propped up on a collection of pillows in the corner as her eyes fluttered shut, and her breath grew steady and peaceful, a shadowy figure stood over her small frame in the dark. I tried to rise, but my body was filled with a heavy numbness, and I succumbed to the darkness of sleep.

Chapter Thirteen

My haze of slumber was torn apart by a thunderous crash and a gut-wrenching screech that ripped through the calm of the morning.

My eyes shot open, and I was on my feet before the tingle of sleep had left my limbs. I scanned the room, fists clenched and ready for a fight, to find Lilian, her serene face now twisted into a mask of fury, standing in the kitchen with her hands wrapped around Iona's throat. Iona dangled off the ground, her hysteric kicks failing to break free from Lilian's vice-like hold.

Beside me, from our makeshift beds on the floor, Gelis shot up, eyes bulging in terror. Without hesitation, we lunged forward, grappling with Lilian's thrashing form, desperate to pry her fingers from Iona's neck.

"You took it you evil woman!" Lilian's voice ricocheted through the room, primal and guttural. Spittle flew from her lips in frenzied bursts, and her eyes bulged with madness as she raged against our grasp.

Iona's gasps were drowned out by the ugly sobs wracking her body. Streams of salty tears poured down her blotched face connecting with the drool pooling at her chin.

"I don't know what you're talking about! I..." Iona wheezed.

But her denial was cut short as Lilian thrust forward once more, sending Gelis and me crashing into a shelf of pots. The metal containers tumbled down around us with a deafening roar.

"Lilian, what the hell are you doing?" I yelled, trying to pin her arms behind her back as she writhed and twisted as if possessed.

"Let me go!" she growled through gritted teeth.

A loud knocking reverberated through the room, and we all stopped our scuffling, looking to the door. It crashed open with a forceful thud, and a muscly, bearded man crowded the doorway, his hands clenched and the veins of his forearms bulging.

"What is the meaning of this?" he bellowed, his deep voice reverberating off the walls like thunder.

"M-M-Mr. MacCaffery," Iona sobbed.

A small, pregnant woman appeared behind him, squeezing her way past the bullish man and rushing to Iona's side.

"Iona, are you okay? Who are these people?" She trembled with concern as she placed one hand on the floor and the other on her rounded belly, pushing herself to her knees with a grimace. With gentle hands, she pulled Iona close, cradling her sobbing form against her.

"We were arriving for my appointment, and we heard the screaming. We came as quickly as we could," Mrs. MacCaffery said into Iona's hair.

Iona could only sob, her mouth gaping open in anguish as she buried her face in the woman's bosom.

Sensing that our grip on her had loosened, Lilian shook Gelis and me off and stomped toward Iona and Mrs. MacCaffery. With a trembling finger, she pointed accusingly at Iona. Her eyes, usually so calm, now blazed with an unfamiliar fire.

"Do not touch that woman," Lilian spat, her voice laced with venom. "She is a liar and a thief, and she cannot be trusted."

Mrs. MacCaffery pulled Iona nearer, shielding her from Lilian's accusatory leer. With a defiant glare, she responded, "She is a saint, Iona is. When I was first with child, I was so sick I could not move. I was delirious with infection and could neither eat nor drink. Iona saved me, and we are here for our treatment. She is a good woman, and you are to leave this place at once."

Lilian's expression darkened as she advanced closer, her eyes smoldering with accusation.

"No," she growled, choking down a sinister snigger. "She is no saint. She poisoned me, she stole from me. She is vile. She is wicked. Give it back to me you little witch!" she screamed, her words ringing through the room like a curse, her body palpitating with fury.

Lilan's face dropped as her anger was replaced with instant regret "No! I didn't mean..." she began but the damage was done. Mrs. MacCaffery went still, her eyes stretched and dilated in terror as she shoved Iona away, scrambling backward across the floor.

"A witch!" Mr. MacCaffery bayed as he marched toward Iona, his massive boots pounding against the wooden floorboards. "You know what we do to your kind around here," he spat as he seized Iona by the back of her neck, wrenching her around to face him. Rage flushed over his chiseled features; his teeth bared in a wild snarl. "What did you do to my wife witch!?"

"No-nothing Mr. MacCaffery, I'm no witch, you know me," Iona pleaded, kicking her legs in open air.

Mr. MacCaffery reeled back his fist and landed a heavy blow to the side of Iona's head. She fell to the floor with a sickening thud as Mr. MacCaffery drew back again.

Gelis and I launched toward Mr. MacCaffery, but he shook us off with a violent roar. In the distance, voices of men lingered on the air drawn by the screams and chaos.

Lilian's body went rigid with shock, her eyes widening as she turned to us. Utter horror plastered itself on her face as the consequence of her words sank in.

"Run!" Gelis's voice pierced the air.

"Run!" Lilian parroted.

And we ran.

I cast one final look as Mr. MacCaffery dealt another blow and Iona's lifeless figure twitched under the impact. *He's going to kill her*, I thought as I turned my back and fled, the word "witch" still lingering in the air like a sinister shadow.

Chapter Fourteen

We bolted out the door and sprinted down the narrow path back toward the road.

Gelis led the way, her feet kicking up clouds of dust as she moved like a gazelle across the road. We ran until sweat soaked our necks and formed clammy bibs at our collars. We ran until the cries of Mrs. MacCaffery pleading with her husband to stop no longer echoed through the recess of our mind. We ran until the houses disappeared entirely and we were back on a narrow path that weaved its way through a temperate rainforest.

Here, Gelis collapsed, falling to her knees and gasping for air. A scratching wheeze escaped her mouth with each exhale as she looked at Lilian, who leaned against a tree, legs shaking.

"You know not what you have done," Gelis glowered, betrayal etched across her face. "You have condemned her to death!" Her face flushed red, and an angry purple vein bulged from her neck.

Lilian panted, her breath hitching as she swallowed a sob.

"What were you thinking?" I pleaded, running my hands over my head.

"She stole it, and I panicked!" Lilian wailed.

"Stole what?" I asked. I let go of my hair and reached out for my friend. She pushed me away and collapsed into a quaking heap on the ground. Her wails pierced the air, unbridled and ruthless, echoing like the cries of an injured animal caught in a trap.

"The book..." she choked out. "The spellbook... she took it."

"You said you didn't have it."

Lilian scrambled to her feet, now reaching for me, clawing in desperation at my hands and clutching them to her chest. "I wanted to keep you safe. I wrestled it from Lizzy during the scuffle—that's how I got the black eye. I've had it all along. I kept it hidden because I didn't know where Lizzy was, and I was afraid." She looked to Gelis. "I sewed it into the hem of this dress while you two were asleep. It was to protect you." She searched my face for understanding.

I pulled away from her and turned my back. Lilian may be cold and distant, but she was always honest. The sting of betrayal poured down my throat like poison, souring my stomach.

"I knew I shouldn't have met with Lizzy; I should have known better... I just thought that after all these years..." Lilian grumped, tucking her hands under her elbows.

I pivoted on my heels to face Lilian, my expression hardening.

"What do you mean after all *these* years? You know her?" I whispered.

Lilian sighed, her desperation returning. Her words were childlike and lonely. "It feels like a lifetime ago. She was a fellow student during my master's program. Our paths crossed frequently because we were both fascinated by European witch trials. She had this incredible, magnetic charm that pulled people toward her, like moths to a flame. Meanwhile, I lingered on the fringes, completely invisible. I longed to be her friend, and as fate would have it, one day, she approached me. She said 'I've heard our research is similar. Do you want to hang out sometime and talk shop?'" Lilian said, sharpening her voice to mimic Lizzy's shrill tone. "I felt so... appreciated. This popular, beautiful woman wanted to be MY friend. Do you know what that's like, Edgar? To be an outcast and then suddenly embraced by someone like her? I would have done anything to stay in her light. I sidelined my own work to help her succeed, to bask in her presence. But over time, subtle signs of something darker began to surface. She started showing up unannounced at my house, ranting about a woman she found in the archives that she believed she was her ancestor. She was convinced this woman was speaking to her in dreams, telling her witchcraft was real, and that she could corroborate it if she located an old book. She demanded I help her."

"It soon became suffocating, and I had to speak to our advisor about her well-being. When the professor approached her, she was furious with me. she said I ruined everything, made up horrible rumors about me, and then she vanished from school." Lilian hugged herself tighter. "A few months ago she called me. She apologized for the awful things she did, and she sounded so much better. She claimed she had a mental breakdown from the stress of research but said she had gotten care and was returning to finish her thesis. She wanted me to review some archival documents, and I was sucked right back in. I told her you and I would meet her, but she insisted I come alone. When I got there, she had a page from the book. She said she was still studying the woman, but no longer believed she was speaking to her in dreams. She said that the book could be proof that some women were practicing healing medicine and that their records could have been the reason for their accusations. She made me feel special all over again, praising my work and telling me there was nobody else she trusted to help with such a momentous discovery. She said we could find the book together and maybe co-publish the findings.

"You don't understand, Edgar." She gripped her hands together as if it could anchor her swirling emotions. "You have no idea how lonely it is to be me." She glanced around, as if expecting the surrounding landscape to echo the cruel whispers she had endured. "Do you think I don't hear what they say?" Her voice broke, each word a fragile step on a cracking ice. "Someone like her..." she began, "could change everything. She could make people see me differently... She could make me see myself differently." A single tear slid down her cheek. "For once, I wanted to feel like I belonged."

"So, all this time... you lied to me?" My insides were a tangled mess. Not just because she had deceived me, but because I had been there for her, disregarding what anyone else thought and she hadn't even noticed. I had spent countless moments trying to make her feel valued and appreciated, pouring every piece of me into our friendship, and none of it mattered. I shook my head, a bitter smile playing at my lips. "I was always there, Lilian. I liked you for who you are, not for who you were trying to be. Did that mean nothing to you?" My voice cracked, raw emotion breaking through my composure. Grief quickly turned to anger, and I advanced toward her, my body towering over her small frame, smothering her in my massive shadow. I studied her face. The gold sparkle in her eyes, once familiar and comforting, now seemed foreign and unsettling. After years of friendship, I was staring into the eyes of a stranger.

Betrayal coursed through me, searing and relentless, leaving me hollow and breathless. It wasn't just the lie—it was the calculated deception. Her selfish behavior had led me far from home and into this mess. I had trusted her completely, followed her blindly, and now I was adrift in the wrong timeline and more alone than I could have ever imagined. In this moment, I could only blame her, the friend I thought I knew.

"You're despicable," I spat, my words dripping with venom. "Pretentious," I dug deeper. "And apparently violent. You only care about research. You don't care about anyone but yourself, and you lie to the only person on this planet who can tolerate you. You're a terrible friend and maybe an even worse person," I snapped, the words lingering between us heavy and final. Across from me, her face paled.

I turned my back and walked away.

As I stalked deeper into the forest each step felt like trudging through quicksand. My own harsh words weighed me down. The distant figures of Lilian and Gelis had vanished, swallowed by the clusters of lichen dangling from goat willow trees. I was alone with only the rattle in my brain and a swirling cloud of biting midges.

My thoughts drifted between truths.

I was too harsh—but Lilian lied.

She didn't deserve that—but she *lied*.

I shouldn't have left her—but I couldn't face her now.

The forest felt like a living prison, its towering trees looming over me, their serpentine branches pointing their accusing limbs. Never had I felt so guilty. Never had I felt so alone.

I sank to the ground, hugging my knees to my chest.

A sudden crack rang through the stillness, jolting me from my spiraling introspection. Gelis emerged from a clump of pines, swiping at the tiny clusters of insects swirling around her head.

"She's not with me," she stated, taking another swat at the air.

"Off to destroy more women's lives," I sulked, disdain dripping from my words.

"Quite the contrary," Gelis huffed. "She's off to try and save the life of the woman she wronged. She also asked me to apologize to you," she added, her tone gentle but firm. "I know you're hurt by what she revealed, but if you ever see her again, you should apologize, too. You had every right to be angry, but you had no right to say the things you did. Lilian is different, you and I both know that, and your words will weigh on her forever. She will feel that more than you and I would, and it will rage within her much, much longer. If I were you, I'd be praying for her return so you don't have to live with that being your last conversation on your conscience forever."

Her words pierced through my indignation, igniting a pang of guilt. I had lashed out in anger, unleashing words that cut deeper than intended. I hung my head, unable to meet Gelis's eyes.

"We... We should go back for her," I murmured, my mind replaying our last encounter, each recollection bringing a fresh wave of regret.

"No, we should not," Gelis retorted, resolute. "What she has done, only she can fix. And it is easier for one person to mask themselves than for three. Her accusations will ignite a storm in that village, and they will look for us. But alone, she can conceal herself."

I sighed, shifting my weight from one foot to the other. "Well, what are we to do then?"

"We shall travel to the Capital," Gelis declared. "Lilian says she will try to help Iona and then reconnect with us in the city, God willing."

With a heavy heart, I nodded in agreement. Our journey was far from over.

Chapter Fifteen

Lilian

His words echoed through my soul like an off-key note in an empty room.

I've always known I'm not the easiest person to tolerate, let alone love. Everyone who came into my life would eventually leave and it was always my fault. Family or friend, it all ends the same. Patience wears thin, their warmth turns to cold, then the inevitable would happen they'd distance themselves and eventually desert me. The first time it happened I was a teen, and the separation was from my mother. She would always jest about my peculiarities, teasing me about my knack for being... well, intolerable and I'd chuckle along, unaware of the weight her words carried. I know she loved me, but I often wondered if she did so out of obligation rather than genuine affection. I never quite fit the mold she envisioned for her ideal life, and my quirks often clashed with her picture-perfect image, so she became more distant, a mother only in name. When I left for university she did not stand in the driveway and wave me off with a hanky in hand. She was relieved, and I could see the weight lift from her shoulders as I drove away. I never went back. It was easier for her this way.

I understand it though. I've always been peculiar, an oddity in a world that craves conformity. The truth is, I've always felt like a misfit puzzle piece, a little off-kilter and always trying to fit in. My mind operates on a different wavelength, and I am hyper-aware of it. It makes every social interaction feel like I'm navigating a labyrinth blindfolded. To be truthful, most days I can barely tolerate myself.

But Edgar—sweet Edgar—saw something in me that others didn't. He saw beyond my awkward facade and embraced the tangled mess beneath, and I had thrown it all away because I was too oblivious to see it.

I have always admired him, and perhaps I should have shared that more. Before he began his tenure at Oxford, I had taken it upon myself to review his dissertation. He was insightful, thorough, and even a little bit witty, which is a challenging thing to accomplish in a thesis.

When we met for the first time at a fundraising event, I wanted to match his wit, but in true Lilian fashion, I blew it. I still remember the way his face fell when I joked that he was stalking me. I had rehearsed our meeting and my jokes so many times that I had no other way to go but headfirst into my bit. So I did. Doubling down on the "joke" until all eyes were on us. By the time I realized the error of my ways it was too late. I still cringe at the memory.

Thankfully, he was forgiving, though I believe the poem I gifted him helped. I've never told him, but it took me months to locate that and cost quite a sum to acquire it from a private collection. I was so fascinated by his research that I had done a deep dive into *The Brollachan* after I read it. I intended to use the poem as an icebreaker when he started, but after my display of ineptitude at our first meeting, I believed the only way to salvage any form of civility between us was to gift it to him. I don't regret it. He cherishes it. It sits as a point of pride in his office, and every time he looks at it, that same beautiful, creeping softness crosses his face. A softness I would never see again.

Edgar... oh Edgar, if only you knew. After our first awkward meeting I found myself staring blankly at my work, your smile intruding on my thoughts. Your friendship was the light that made all my days brighter and I hate myself for driving it away.

I will miss the way you'd laugh at my terrible attempts at humor, and the way your eyes crinkle at the corners when you're deep in concentration. I will miss our late-night conversations, where time seemed to stand still, but most of all, I will just miss you, desperately, more than I thought possible. I will regret forever my own mistakes, knowing I've pushed away the one person who truly saw me.

And then there was Iona. Violence is not something I'm prone to, but in moments of sweltering emotion, I become a slave to my impulses. When I woke to find the book missing, I quite literally saw red. My memories of the morning have waxed and waned through my mind, snippets of a horror show that make my skin grow clammy and cold.

I had ruined everything.

In the moments after Edgar stormed off, anguish etched on his face like so many before him. Gelis, bless her heart, offered me the grace I didn't deserve. She swooped in and wrapped me in her arms. As usual, my body stiffened at her touch—I never have managed to grasp the societal norm of hugs. Yet, despite my response, in Gelis's warm hold I found a fleeting sense of solace. While I stood rigid as a board in her embrace, a tumult of emotions swirled inside of me, and while I had the strong urge to do so, I couldn't muster a tear.

Why? Because in many ways, Edgar was right. I struggle to see beyond the confines of my own mind, which is perpetually consumed by information, research, nagging self-hatred and a perpetual static buzz. It is loud in my head and I get lost in it easily, often forgetting there is a world with other people outside the space between my ears.

It's not that I don't try to consider how my actions affect others; I do, it's just that sometimes I struggle to comprehend it all. How is one supposed to deal with the incessant hum of their own mind while also nurturing others around them? It is hard, but I am always trying, even though most times I fail. While he is right about many things, there is one thing Edgar got wrong. I do care about others—a lot. I care about Gelis and what she thinks of me after my outburst. I care about Iona and the abuse she has sustained because of my thoughtlessness. But most of all, I care about Edgar, all of him, more than I've ever cared about anyone else.

Which is exactly why I lied.

I could see the admiration in Edgar's eyes when he looked at me, an awe that made me feel both cherished and guilty. His gaze was always filled with a quiet reverence, as if I were something precious and unblemished. It was that very look that made me want to protect the idealistic image he had of me. I couldn't bear to shatter that illusion, to let him see the flaws and insecurities

I tried so hard to hide. If he knew that beneath the surface his friend was actually desperate for acceptance, I feared it would shatter his mirage of me and I would become—like I have to so many others—an annoying inconvenience requiring comfort and support instead of something to be revered.

I pinched the bridge of my nose. "You idiot."

Letting Lizzy back into my life was a mistake—I see that now. But she was the only one I had a genuine connection with before Edgar. When she reappeared, her smile as bright and wild as ever, I dared to hope that maybe, just maybe, she had changed from the maniacal, troubled person I once knew. Compared to Edgar's steady, unwavering friendship, Lizzy's presence was a storm. Yet, I wished for a world where both could coexist, where Lizzy's chaotic brilliance wouldn't overshadow the quiet light Edgar brought into my life, and I could have two friends, for once in my lonely life.

I am pathetic.

As I loitered on the fringes of Iona's village, I forced my self-loathing to the back of my mind. Now wasn't the time for self-pity; it was a time for focus. It was imperative I channeled my brain's laser-like intensity into finding a solution to the mess I had created—a solution that might free Iona from certain death.

Sticking to the outskirts where the houses were sparse, I moved through the bushels of cowberry that encircled the community. The broad, leafy bushes provided cover as I navigated the shadows. I peered over the paddocks surrounding each home, scanning for a disguise, acutely aware that my bright dress would make me an easy target for the man and the pregnant woman who had appeared at Iona's door.

"*MacCaffery!*" Iona's scream echoed in my mind, cutting and clear. "*Mr. MacCaffery,*" she cried out as my hands tightened around her windpipe. The sudden recollection hit me like a blow, twisting my stomach into knots. I shook my head, dragging the memory away.

I had to stay alert, unseen, and keep moving.

On the horizon, a fair distance from the last paddock, stood a small farmhouse, its windows shut against the biting wind. I stopped and squinted in its direction. Along the side of the house a clothesline hung taut between two posts, and a pair of boys' britches and a gray linen shirt flapped wildly, snapping like flags in the breeze.

I moved from the bushes and crouched in the tall grass bordering the property. My breath synced and I began my ritual of internal counting—sixty; counted five times over, then five times more. Ten minutes passed and nobody stirred. It seemed safe to assume the occupants were either gone or preoccupied inside.

I stood and tugged my dress off my shoulders, wriggling against the compressed bodice to free my arms from the sleeves. With my arms finally loose, I rotated the dress so the tightened strings were in front of me, ready to untie. The wind whipped around me, chilling my exposed skin, but I couldn't afford to hesitate. I needed that disguise, and I needed it now.

As I struggled to loosen the binds, memories of Edgar's careful tying of the strings and the tender caress of his touch grazing my skin flooded my mind. My fingers faltered. "Shit," I cursed as I yanked the bodice apart, and the dress fell with a dull thud onto the grass.

Crouching low, exposed but determined, I eyed the clothesline and began a swift, crouched jog toward the house. As I neared the line, I hesitated, scanning my surroundings to ensure the coast was clear. With a quick, decisive move, I darted forward and snatched the goods.

A dog yipped nearby, electrifying my nerves. I sprinted back to the safety of the shadows, clutching the stolen garments. Success.

Safely enclosed in a circle of alders, I began altering the clothes. Not drastically, but enough to avoid suspicion if the owners spotted me. I adjusted the britches and shirt to fit my frame, their bristly fabric itchy and uncomfortable compared to my discarded dress.

Disguise complete.

I plunked down on the ground to relax my heartrate. The trees wrapped around me like a protective cloak, the rustling leaves and skyward bird calls creating a soothing backdrop for my overactive mind. I stretched out on the mossy ground and looked skyward, recapping my plan.

It was straightforward. Step one: Disguise myself as a teenage boy, utilizing my short hair and slender frame to aid the ruse. Check. Step two: Enter the village around dusk and find the local pub where I would listen for gossip about Iona's whereabouts. Step three: Locate her and liberate her.

I propped myself up on my elbows and tilted my head to the side. The plan was simple in theory, but the execution posed challenges, particularly freeing her. As my mind raced through various scenarios, I came to the sobering realization that devising a plan would be pointless without knowledge of her exact location. I would have to wait until that crucial detail was uncovered.

I lay back again with a huff, feeling helpless as I watched the sun dip in the sky. Time dragged on and the forest's dampness seeped into my bones, and I curled into a compact ball, limbs weighed down with weariness. The world slowed as exhaustion enveloped me, my eyelids growing heavy until they fluttered closed, and sleep took over.

I woke to the world around me shrouded in the inky blackness of night. The once cheery chirps of woodland birds had vanished, replaced by the eerie symphony of nature's nocturnal creatures.

My mossy bed had left me surprisingly refreshed and alert as I sat up and took a moment to gather my bearings. The cool, damp air clung to my skin, and I shivered involuntarily.

With an awkward stumble, I rose from my makeshift bed, brushing off the remnants of the forest floor that clung to my clothes. I took one final, critical assessment of my disguise. My clothes were damp and speckled with dirt, but that seemed fitting for a traveling man.

I shimmied, my arms and legs waggling as I tried to shake off the unease that gnawed at the edges of my consciousness. The path ahead was uncertain, but the possibility of answers drove me forward. Civilization awaited, but so did the dangers and challenges that came with it. I was ready to face them, to save Iona, whatever the cost.

Chapter Sixteen

The distant echoes of spirited chatter reached my ears long before the village came into view. As I drew nearer, the flickering glow of oil lamps illuminated the cobblestone streets, expelling dancing shapes against the rickety facades of the buildings.

Among the darkened homes, one beacon of light beckoned—a modest building heaving with raucous laughter.

"That's got to be the pub," I said aloud.

I approached with a steadying breath and positioned myself at the entrance, steeling my nerves for the charade I was about to undertake. Tonight, I would become Jasper Mar, a young man of humble origins seeking shelter and employment in exchange for honest labor. I adjusted my garments and tousled my hair, rehearsing the fabricated details of my backstory one final time. Every aspect of my tale had to be plausible and unremarkable for this to work.

"Ok, you can do this," I said to myself, pumping my fists in the air.

I plastered a mealymouthed grin onto my face and swung the door open.

The tavern's interior was bathed in a warm, orange haze cast by the crackling fire and the oil lamps. Beads of sweat instantly broke out at my hairline, a combination of the unbearable heat and the sudden attention that descended on me as I entered the establishment.

A hush fell over the room silencing the lively banter from moments before. Every eye turned toward me, their gazes like needles piercing my core. My heart quickened as I made my way to the unpolished wooden bar, each footstep thundering in the uneasy quiet.

Behind the bar stood the proprietor, a short old woman with a weary countenance. Her auburn hair was swirled with streaks of rosy white. Her face was plump and cherubic, with kind features and a flippant upturned nose which was dripping with beads of sweat as she ran a stained grey cloth across the bar top, oblivious to the fact that she was merely spreading the sloshed ale around rather than cleaning it. I suppressed the urge to comment on the futility of her efforts, reminding myself that I was no longer Lilian but Jasper—a sixteen-year-old boy who wouldn't make such observations.

"Ahem," I sounded.

The barmaid ignored me and continued her task of wiping.

I took one step closer and placed my palms in the space she was wiping.

"Pardon me, but might ye' have lodgin' available? I've nae got a penny to my name, but I'm willing to work hard and lend a hand," I said in my rehearsed Lowland accent.

She stopped her cleaning and raised an eyebrow at me.

"Where's yer' ma, lad?" she inquired, her drawl so thick my brain had to work overtime to understand her.

"Dead, along with my father," I replied, casting my gaze downward and wrapping my arms around myself in a pretense of grief.

The hardness in her face dissolved and she abandoned the rag on the countertop.

"And how old might ye' be, son?" she asked, her voice calm and comforting.

"Sixteen," I responded, my pulse pounding in my eardrums.

She tilted her head downward, scrutinizing my features, before eventually nodding. "Aye. It's yer lucky day," she declared, her voice raspy from years in the stale, smoky bar. "Our last bar boy left not long ago—caught him with his hands where they shouldn't be. Ye ain't a thief, are ye ma boy?"

"No ma'am," I said, shaking my head. "Just wanting housing until I can make my way up north tae ma aunt."

She nodded again.

"You can have the bed in the back," she said, tossing me the rag that reeked of stale ale and mildew. I curled my nose and held it in front of me, dangling it between two fingers.

"But right now, you clean the bar. These folk are makin' a right mess of my fine establishment."

She shot a threatening glance at the leering crowd, and suddenly all eyes averted from me, the crackling energy of conversation reigniting across the tavern.

The barmaid kneeled with a groan and scooped up a leaky bucket that she dropped with a thud on the counter, its murky contents sloshing over its sides. I began the arduous task of polishing the filthy wood.

I worked slowly, beginning at the furthest point of the bar top—which was also the furthest point from the patrons. At first, the chatter among the guests was hesitant, as if they were wary of engaging with a newcomer in their midst. But as the evening wore on and the ale flowed constant, they grew rowdier and their inhibitions were lowered.

I had reached the end of the bar, nearer to the crowds, when I finally heard what I had been waiting for: "Iona."

My muscles tensed, but I dared not turn around. I turned my attention to a stubborn stain while straining to hear every slurred word of the speaker.

An old man, his hair flecked with grey, and his nose swollen and veiny from years of excessive consumption, teetered on the edge of his seat. His mug of amber ale sloshed over the rim, landing in the man's lap beside him.

"Iona"— he sniffed— "I always knew the lass was a bit peculiar, but never did I reckon her a witch. But young Robert MacCaffery swears he saw it with his own two eyes," he slurred, jabbing a fat, grimy finger at his companion. "He an' his wife stumbled upon the scene—said they were out for a walk to ease his poor wife's pain when they heard a racket from 'er cottage. He ran ta' see if he could help an' found two women and a giant of a man seeking the services of the witch. But things went awry they did. One of the women turned on Iona, accusing her of heresy. And then— as MacCaffery tells it, Iona changed right before their eyes. 'Er face melted away, and hooves, like those of the devil himself, sprung from her feet. The others fled, when they heard Iona's neighbors approach - the cowards, but MacCaffery, being the strapping fella he is, fought off the devil himself until reinforcements arrived and brought Iona to town. By the time they turned up, she reverted to her proper form—though he swears it the truth that she had cloven hooves."

My hands trembled at this egregious lie. MacCaffery and his wife weren't merely passersby—they were there to seek Iona's services. I dunked the smelly rag into the bucket, but my nerves betrayed me, and it toppled off the bar top with a clatter.

"Shit," I cursed as the attention of the drunk man and his companion shot to me.

The drunk man stood, his eyes glossy and his footing unsteady as he approached.

"Somethin' about that story ya reckon isn't true?" he sneered.

"No, sir," I responded, shaking my head and retrieving the bucket and rag from the floor. "I just didn't know there were witches about—bit frightening isn't it?"

The old drunkard laughed uproariously and thumped me hard on the back, sending the bucket flying back to the floor.

"Don't you worry, lad—she's not the first witch here, but she will be the last. We know how ta' deal with witches in these parts."

He wrapped his arm around my shoulder, pulling me closer, the stench of stale liquor seeping from his pores.

"Well, that's good to know. What do you do with a witch?" I asked, trying to appear innocent in my questioning.

He hugged me tighter.

"She's down at the church now, lad," he sputtered, his words slurred. "Locked up and guarded in the cellar. She'll be allowed ta' confess and atone her sins and renounce her dealings with the devil."

"What if she's innocent though," I asked innocently, rounding my eyes with childlike curiosity.

"She'll confess." He leaned in, eyes glinting with malice. "And if she don't... We have the screws to help her along." He slapped my back, and burst into raucous laughter, spittle flying from his lips and landing on my cheek. "Rest assured lad, we'll get a confession, and the witch will never set a free foot in our village again, and Mr. MacCaffery will get a hero's welcome for ridding our village of evil." He stumbled back to his companion.

A slow, relentless creep of discomfort filled my mouth with saliva. I gulped to push it back down. I had read this narrative hundreds—if not thousands—of times in the annals of history, but now I was witnessing firsthand how one act—MY act could spiral into an accusation and then morph into a grotesque distortion of truth as it spread through the community like a disease.

I covered my mouth with my fist and pushed down a retch at the thought of MacCaffery and his wife, their scowls swirling with glee as they embellished the events for their own selfish gain. The image of Iona, trapped and defenseless in the cold depths of the church cellar, was unbearable. What sickened me most was that I, the distinguished researcher, had set this tragedy in motion. The weight of the blame pressed down on me, a heavy, inescapable burden.

As the evening wore on and the last of the villagers stumbled out into the night clinging to one another for support, I tidied the remnants of spilled booze and vomit that had amassed on the tables. Exhaustion settled over me like a leaden cloak and I collapsed into a stool, my head dropping into my folded arms.

"Leave that for the morning," the barwoman said from her place behind the bar.

I didn't move.

The barwoman moved toward me, her apron swishing, and grabbed me by the hand. She steered me to the back of the bar into a small storage room with a hay mattress on the floor. My weary legs were heavy as lead as I fell in line behind her.

"You'll sleep here," she cooed. "And in the morning, you can finish the cleanup."

Her words were soft and kind—and a new guilt ate away at me, for I knew that when morning came, I would be far from this place, leaving her to tend to the mess herself.

Chapter Seventeen

I lay in the darkness, waiting for the barkeep to finish her rounds.

The room spun as my thoughts churned with manic desperation. I punched the side of my head, trying to silence the chaos within. I had no idea where the church was—the key to Iona's salvation—and no plan to free her from her captors. My heart pounded erratically; each beat a reminder of the potential failure looming over me. The weight of knowing the horrors she faced was making it hard to breath.

The tavern creaked as the old proprietor shuffled across the aged floorboards and locked the front door. Her footsteps lumbered up the stairs and were followed by a voluminous thud as she settled into bed. Soon, the chamber vibrated with her rumbling snores, and I stood, treading on tiptoe as I slipped out the back door.

Outside, the air hung heavy with moisture, and the rickety houses' windows leered down at me like hollow sockets. I crept down the street, peering down each narrow alleyway in search of Iona.

The chill of the night bit into my skin as I turned corner after corner on the unfamiliar streets, my eyes scanning the horizon for a shadowed steeple or cross.

Then came the sound. Roaring through the empty street—guttural and horrifying, like a feral animal in a trap. Agonizing screams pierced through the stillness, each cry coiling around my insides.

"Iona," I whispered as I broke into a frenzied sprint, my pulse pounding as images of Iona's torment flashed behind my eyes.

"Oh, dear God, please let me not arrive too late," I prayed.

Her cries grew louder, each one a haunting crescendo that spurred me forward. I rounded one final corner and climbed a steep hill, my calves burning with exertion and there, looming over me like a malevolent specter, stood the church—a grotesque parody of sanctity, witness to unspeakable horrors.

Its stone walls were constructed of dark granite and adorned with intricate carvings of Celtic knots. The steeple's pitched roof was covered in slate and topped with a simple iron cross weathered by centuries of wind and rain.

Every creak of my footsteps echoed in the stillness of the night as I neared the main doors. Iona's fate hinged on my ability to keep my fear in check, to blend into the background without alerting those who guarded her. My knees knocked together as I climbed the deteriorating steps. I reached out, my fingers atremble as they closed around the brass knob and twisted. It turned easily, and the door swung open without noise, revealing a cavernous interior bathed in ghostly grey light.

I advanced on my tiptoes to limit the echo of my feet on the old flagstone floors and surveyed my surroundings. Rows of plain wooden pews faced the chancel where a simple altar stood draped in a faded cloth. The walls were adorned with biblical frescos, their colors muted from the passage of time. In my other life, this chapel would have ignited a frenzy of exhilaration, but now the colossal wooden cross that dominated the altar and projected elongated shadows across the vacant pews caused beads of anxious sweat to pool on my forehead.

The air stank of incense and the unmistakable, rusty tang of blood, sticky and suffocating. A wave of nausea swept over me as I threw my hands to my mouth to stop myself from gagging.

"Do you deny the accusations brought against you lass? That you consort with dark forces and practice witchcraft?" the interrogator's voice boomed through the room. I dove behind the altar and curled into a tight ball.

"I am no witch. I'm just a simple woman who tends to my gardens and helps mothers bring wee ones into the world," Iona's pleading floated up from below. The drunkards were right. Her voice was coming from the basement. I rolled over and pressed my ear to the floor.

"Enough of your lies, witch!" the interrogator roared, followed by the sickening thud of fists on flesh and a yelp of anguish from Iona. "Confess your sins and repent, or face the consequences of your wickedness!"

"I will confess nothing," Iona quivered. "For I have done nothing wrong."

The interrogator emitted a primal roar, his rage a seismic wave that caused the floorboards to quake.

The chamber was then enveloped in violence, overflowing with the sickening sounds of impact. Each blow landed like meat being tenderized and was escorted by Iona's anguished cries. The relentless onslaught continued, a symphony of brutality that resonated off the walls until I could stand it no more.

I had no plan, but if I didn't act now, Iona would be dead before morning.

I uncurled myself and searched the space, my eyes eventually resting on a winding staircase spiraling downward to the torture chamber below.

I ran toward the steps, but as my toes hit the top of the landing, a shadowy profile materialized, clamping a hand over my mouth and dragging me back.

I struggled against the suffocating clutch of my assailant, my limbs thrashing in a crazed bid for freedom. My heart hammered against my ribcage, and desperation clawed at me as my mind raced with the terrifying possibilities of what awaited me, the worst of which that I would never see Edgar again.

My captor's hold tightened, shaking me with urgency. A breathy voice tickled my ear, "If you promise not to yell, I will uncover your mouth—but you must *promise*. We will both be in grave danger if you even squeak."

It was a woman's voice, her Scottish accent coloring each word with a lilt of the Highlands.

I nodded and the hand over my mouth slowly withdrew. She turned me to face her, her features emerging from the shadows like a ghostly apparition. Her finger pressed against her lips in a plea for silence.

Mrs. Robert MacCaffery.

She was still marked by the weight of an impending due date and the swell of her belly caused a persistent sway in her stance. Her lips turned downward in a perpetual frown, and her face was puffy either from crying or pregnancy—I wasn't sure which.

Her fingers curled around my arm, dragging me deeper into the murky recesses of the hallway above the stairwell. In the darkness, her hand found mine, our fingers intertwining in a powerful clasp. With a shaky point of her available hand, she directed my gaze to the basement, muffled sounds of struggle echoed up the stairs.

"Come, you vile woman," a venomous voice spat.

Iona whimpered, her frantic steps faltering as she scrambled upward.

The man materialized first, a towering figure with fiery red hair and a bushy beard that consumed his face. His trousers were stained deep burgundy with blood, and his breath came in ragged gasps of rage.

Mr. Robert MacCaffery.

MacCaffery's left hand extended behind him, tangled in Iona's hair, now a mess of matted strands and streaks of crimson.

As he hauled her upwards, Iona's hair slipped from her face, her once gentle features now a marred canvas of maroon and blue bruises. One eye had swollen shut, and blood was trickling from a split lip. Every movement seemed to cause her discomfort, and her clothes were torn and stained. She tried to stand and turn herself, but her legs buckled under her, her body contorting in agony.

I lunged forward, but Mrs. MacCaffery's grip tightened like a vice, crushing my fingers together with a searing pain that threatened to buckle my knees.

I turned to her, pleading for release, wrenching at Iona's torment. She shook her head, her eyes overflowing with terror.

So we stayed hidden, as Mr. MacCaffery drag the battered and bloodied Iona across the creaking floorboards and out into the night. Her vacant eyes, once full of life, now stared with a ghoulish emptiness at the crucifix on the wall, silently pleading for salvation as her body fell limp in the grasp of her captor.

In the darkness outside, MacCaffery's voice was joined by a chorus of violent, leering men. Their footsteps and mocking jeers haunted the air long after they vanished into the shadowy night.

When their voices had faded Mrs. MacCaffery released my hand. "He's taking her to the Capital, to the Court of the Justiciary," she sputtered.

Her eyes welled up, brimming with unshed tears that sparkled like dewdrops on a morning leaf. "After you left, he dragged her outside and beat her mercilessly. I tried to stop him, but he shoved me to the ground. Then the neighbors arrived, and they just kept beating her and beating her. I was frightened when you said Iona was a witch, but what they have accused her of isn't true. I was there when they brought her into town, parading her like a prized stallion bruised and bullied. As the crowds gathered so did his confidence and he began spewing all sorts of absurdities about her turning into the devil. I was so shocked that I couldn't muster a word. I just stood there like a frump and let him lie." She paced back and forth across the floorboards, which creaked and groaned with each step. "When we got home, I asked why he lied, and he said that our visits to Iona were growing too expensive, that if I were a real woman I could birth this child without the extra expense. I couldn't believe it. The man I had married, being so unkind about my discomfort. I followed him here tonight with the plan to free Iona, whatever the cost, but as I listened to the evil grow in his voice, I lost my courage. If I tried to intervene he wouldn't just kill Iona, he'd kill me and my wee one too."

The horror in her eyes mirrored the terror in my heart. Every word painted a vivid picture of the brutality Iona had endured and the torment that awaited her in Edinburgh.

"Then I saw you...I recognized you. "Her jaw tightened. "If you're here you know she's innocent too," she said, grabbing my hands and pulling me close. "How can I bring a child into this world knowing its father is a monster? That he is responsible for the abuse of an innocent and good woman?" Her shoulders began to convulse.

I paused, then pulled her to me, wrapping my arms around her. She buried her face in my chest, her bleats soaking through my shirt. The intensity of her pain reverberated through me, vibrating my collarbone.

"Oh, Mrs. MacCaffery, I am so sorry," I whispered into her ear. "I am so sorry for causing this. I was angry because Iona stole a book from me, but I never meant for this to happen. The words I spoke were born of my own pain. I beg you to forgive me for causing you and your little one any harm."

She pulled away, holding me at arm's length.

"Then save her," she said. "Make it right."

CHAPTER EIGHTEEN

In the subdued light of the church, we clung to each other until the first whispers of dawn trickled through the windows. Two women, practically strangers, bound by a desperate need to save Iona. Mrs. MacCaffery recounted every detail of the events since I accused Iona, her voice trembling. She spoke of how the men planned to transport Iona by wagon to the city and present her to the Court for trial on charges of witchcraft. Mr. MacCaffery and the others planned to testify against her, weaving lies into supposed truths—accusing Iona of transforming into the devil and killing babies in the womb. They had ransacked her cottage and pulled down bundles of herbs that they intended to present as evidence.

"I don't know how I will make it in time," I brooded. "They have a few hours' start on me, and the journey is a long one by foot."

Mrs. MacCaffery's face squared in resolve. "There's an old man down the road named Mr. Beaton. He travels between here and the Burghs most days, taking a horse-drawn carriage with crates of goods to sell. I'll take you to him, and we'll see if you can get a ride. Her voice trembled with remorse. "I wish I could join you, but it would not be safe for me at this stage."

I nodded. "I can manage, Mrs. MacCaffery. And again, I'm sorry."

She turned to me, horizontal wrinkles creasing her brow. "My dear, you've apologized enough to the wrong person. You've done no wrong by me. Your actions have inadvertently shown me the true nature of the man I married, and for that, I am indebted. I am sorry too, for being silent in the face of injustice. I stood there and allowed the accusations to grow, never finding the courage to speak my truth. I will never forgive myself for allowing another woman to suffer."

"It is harder than one thinks to go against the masses," I said. "Don't be too hard on yourself, I will do what I can to save Iona."

"And if something happens to my bastard husband in the process," Mrs. MacCaffery stated. "Well, I can promise there will be no hard feelings."

We left together before the morning bustle of bartering and trade began. Mrs. MacCaffery waddled beside me, each breath a gasp under the burden of her large belly. The journey was brief. Five hundred meters from the church door was a small, ramshackle hut, that creaked violently in the gentle breeze.

"Someone lives here?" I asked, surveying the rotten boards hanging loose from the rafters.

"It's a sad story," Mrs. MacCaffery said as she rapped hard on the door, which hung loose on its hinges and rattled with each knock.

The door opened almost instantaneously.

An old man emerged, hunched at the waist, his back heaving with an ugly lump on the nape of his neck. His white beard reached well below his chin, and the bristly hairs around his mouth were yellowed with age. His watery steel-blue eyes lit up upon seeing Mrs. MacCaffery, and his chapped mouth parted in a mammoth toothless grin.

"My dear," he said, gesturing with arthritic bending hands into his tiny hovel. "Come in."

"It's lovely to see you sir," Mrs. MacCaffery cooed as she strode with purpose into the old man's home.

"You too, lad, come, come, no need to linger out there," he said, placing a hand on my back and giving me a gentle shove inside.

He bustled around the messy one-room hovel, pushing a collection of hand-carved dishes off the unbalanced chair directly onto the floor. "Deal with that later," he muttered as pulled it out for Mrs. MacCaffery. "You must get off your feet, that wee one will be joining us in no time," he grinned, obviously pleased to have company.

Mrs. MacCaffery absentmindedly rubbed her belly. "Mr. Beaton, I cannot stay for long, but I wanted to introduce you to…" Horror devoured her face. Despite our time spent together in the confines of the church, she suddenly realized she had never asked my name.

"Jasper," I interjected, extending a hand to the old man. He seized it and shook it with vigor, his skin translucent like crepe paper, the blue of his veins shining through. "I'm traveling through to the Capital, looking for work," I said, rolling my 'r's with a soft burr. "Met Mrs. MacCaffery here on the road, and she says you may be looking for some company on your journey."

The old man's eyes lit up and he clapped his misshapen hands together. "Aye, son. I'll take you, but you gotta' help me load the cart first!" he said, shuffling to the door.

I looked to Mrs. MacCaffery, who shooed me off after him with a gentle smile.

"All these here need to go" he said, pointing to a teetering stack of splintery wooden crates overflowing with nearly rotted vegetables.

Mrs. MacCaffery, who had waddled her way to the cart with slow and deliberate steps, curled her nose at the pungent aroma.

After the goods were loaded (though certainly not secure), Mr. Beaton, his hands trembling with the rhythmic shake of old age, saddled up his horse, a creature as old and hunched as himself, and I turned to Mrs. MacCaffery.

"I'll find her," I promised, forcing a small, bittersweet smile.

"I know," she replied, swallowing hard.

We lingered in a brief, silent moment, broken only by Mr. Beaton's call.

"Alright, my lad—off we go!"

Mrs. MacCaffery enveloped me in a firm embrace, my small frame pressed against her solid, rounded belly.

"Be safe," she whispered into my ear.

"I will," I answered, though my voice now lacked conviction.

She released me, and I turned back towards the carriage with a final wave.

"Oh! Jasper!" Mrs. MacCaffery's voice called, beckoning me back to her.

I jogged a few paces until I was in front of her again.

"I meant to say, you said earlier that you were angry at Iona because she stole your book. When they went to collect the evidence, those vile men stripped that deprived woman naked and turned the whole place upside down. Not a single book was found."

CHAPTER NINETEEN

I sat facing backward, my eyes fixed on the diminishing outline of Mrs. MacCaffery until she became a speck on the horizon. Her final words reverberated in my mind. *"There was no book to be found."*

It had to be a mistake. The men must have overlooked it. I was certain the book was there when I arrived at Iona's—I had checked the hem of my dress multiple times throughout the day. When it snagged in the woods and Gelis had to free me, paranoia set in. The worry of it falling out consumed me, and I bundled the hem in my hands, reassuring myself it was still safely concealed. I had checked it one last time, moments before slipping into my drug-induced sleep.

I turned back around, shifting my focus to my new companion, hoping that looking ahead and distracting myself would calm the tide of queasiness washing over me from the bumpy, uneven road.

"Thank you again," I said.

"Not a worry, Jasper," he said with a smile. "Always happy to have company on this road. It can be a long jaunt with just ol' Frances for company," he added, leaning forward to pat the old horse affectionately on her backside.

"So..." I hesitated, struggling to continue the conversation. "What... What are you selling?"

He chuckled. "You saw what I was selling, boy. Anything the village folk will part with. The Capital's been bustling these past few years. People moving there en masse. They'll buy anything, so I round up all sorts and take it down there—most days I come back with some coins in my pocket and a much lighter load." He shifted in his seat. "So, what's your story?" he asked, eyeing me with suspicion. "What's a young fella like you doing out looking for work?"

"Ma's dead—so's Pa. I have an aunt in the Capital who will let me live there," I said, altering my story slightly.

"Humph," he grumped, chewing at the corner of his lip. "Funny... 'Cause last night in the pub, I heard ya tell ol' Mrs. Bains, the barmaid, that your aunt lived way up north."

"Well..." I stammered. "You see... I..." The realization hit me like a punch to the gut. Mr. Beaton had been there; out of all the scenarios I had bounced around in my brain, this was not one of them. I had never considered the possibility of being overheard—and it seemed now like such an obvious mistake.

His stern voice cut through my looping thoughts. "Look, lad," he said, his eyes narrowing. "I don't care where your aunt lives or if you even have one. But I do care that you're not some criminal planning to rob an old man and leave him for dead. So, why don't you tell me at least a piece of the truth?" His voice wavered. The cost of these journeys was evident in his tired eyes; he was well aware of his age and fragility.

"If I tell you, will you kill me?" I asked, my words faint and fragile.

He chortled a dry, mirthless sound. "Do I look like I could do much in the way of killing? I might throw you off the cart if I can even muster the strength for that," he said, gazing at his own weathered hands on the reins. "But no—killing isn't my way." He concentrated on the road ahead as if inviting my confession.

The words poured out of me like a dam bursting. "I'm not Jasper," I admitted, my fake accent falling away. "I'm actually Lilian, I'm English, and it's my fault that Iona is being taken to the Capital."

Mr. Beaton shrank down in his seat, his eyes never straying from the roadway. I swallowed the lump forming behind my tongue, the story tumbling out in disjointed pieces.

"I was visiting her with a friend of mine and we stayed the night. I woke in the morning to a cherished book missing and I thought she stole it. I lost my temper and said horrible things. I called her a witch, and the MacCaffery's were there. Mr. MacCaffery grabbed her and hit her, and I was so frightened I ran away with my friends. When we stopped to rest after fleeing, my friend called me awful names, and I deserved every one of them. So I left them and came back for Iona. I went to the bar in the hopes of hearing some gossip and I did. I feel bad for leaving the old barmaid high and dry but when that drunkard said she was in the church, well I had to try and save her. When I got there, Mr. MacCaffery was torturing her, and Mrs. MacCaffery told me not to try and save her there, because they would kill me too. We let them leave with her, and then I came to you because Mrs. MacCaffery said you might take me to the Capital so I could try and save her."

The confession left me breathless, but as soon as the last word escaped my lips, I lightened, the burden removed. I glanced fearfully at Mr. Beaton.

"I know Iona," he responded. "When my dear Maeve was ill—that was my wife," he added, casting a look in my direction before turning back to the road. "We went to Iona often. She was the only one who could soothe her suffering." He paused, his eyes distant. "Iona would sit with Maeve in the garden of that wee little cottage. They'd sip a peculiar tea Iona made, one that eased Maeve's discomfort, and gab away for hours. Iona never treated her like she was sick—they were just friends having a cuppa'." He smiled faintly, remembering. "Maeve would chatter all the way back, saying how good the visit was and how much better she felt." He sighed a sorrowful sound. "When Maeve got worse, and we couldn't walk to her anymore, Iona would come to us. She even brought a small potted plant for Maeve to have in the house because she missed sitting in the garden so much." His voice broke, and he wiped at the corner of his eye. "The day I knew Maeve was departing this earth, I sent the neighbor to get Iona. She comforted Maeve through her passing and comforted me in the days afterward. Iona is the reason my wife was able to leave this world in peace."

A small whimper escaped his lips, and he pulled on the reins, stopping the cart and turning to face me. His eyes swam with a mixture of sorrow and regret.

"I wish you hadn't done what you did. Iona is a gift to our community—and now she will never be able to return," he said, his words cutting through me like a knife.

I began to rise, ready to dismount, but his spindly hand reached out and rested on mine.

"But you're trying to right your wrongs," he said, patting my hand. "People who do bad for the sake of doing bad—they don't try to fix it." He looked at me with a spark of tenacity in his eyes. "I'll take you to the Capital, lad." He paused and corrected himself with a small, sad smile. "I mean, lass. And I'll do what I can to help you find our Iona."

Chapter Twenty

The mood between us had lightened as we bumped down the path. Mr. Beaton's demeanor lifted as he regaled me with tales of his late wife, his eyes twinkling with happy memories. We ambled along, passing small villages and rarely meeting other carts, then stopped by a small stream where Frances drank gratefully, and we checked the load.

"This talk of witches isn't new around these parts, you know," Mr. Beaton remarked as he shifted a tipped-over crate of potatoes back to its upright position.

"Iona mentioned that a girl named Angus had been driven away because of accusations," I said, trying to sound nonchalant.

"Ahh yes, Angus. But not just young Angus—another as well, named Isobel."

At the sound of the name, I turned away, shuffling some of the baskets to hide the creeping sense of awareness that was growing within me.

"An odd one, Isobel was," he recalled. "She arrived as a young lass and was always a bit of a mystery. She kept to herself, drifting quietly along the fringes of society. If someone were ill, she'd offer help, but it always came at a cost. Sometimes minor—a meal or lodging. Other times, if the person was desperate, the cost was much greater—fine jewelry, family heirlooms, even a home on the edge of town." He pulled the leather strap meant to secure the load, and it snapped back at him. He growled. "At first, we thought she was just a bit greedy—the people who needed help claimed that the high cost was worth the healing, but then there were the rumors."

He hesitated, questioning if he should continue. I stopped my adjusting and turned my attention to him.

"There was a young mother who went to her for help. Destitute and clutching her feverish child, she knocked at Isobel's door. Isobel asked what she wanted, and the mother explained her child was gravely ill and that she had tried everything. The cost, Isobel said, would be high. The mother, willing to do anything, offered a prized piece of jewelry, but Isobel insisted on something else. About a year later, the child had grown healthy and spry, but the mother deteriorated. She became bony and thin, and her eyes hollowed and grew cavernous black bags under them. She used to be involved in the church but stopped attending; after a while she stopped going into town at all. Her husband would come to the pub at night to gripe about the changes in his wife. He complained that often, when he got home half drunk, she would be gone from the house and the young one would be wailing away alone. She wouldn't return until the early hours of the morning, trying to sneak into bed without him knowing. Then one dawn, she was found in the town center by a shopkeeper arriving for the day. She was sitting cross-legged, with her eyes fixed to the sky, a candle burned almost to the ground in front of her. She was speaking in a language the shopkeeper couldn't understand so he roused the churchmen to come and help her. As the morning light grew, other villagers arrived, but nobody could break her trance. They took her into the church and locked her in the basement. After about a day, she was back to her usual self."

He swallowed hard. "The clergymen asked what she was doing out there, and she confessed to making a deal with Isobel—to rescue her son. She claimed she had to serve Isobel for a year from the date of his healing. Said Isobel had her do all kinds of outrageous things that drained her energy and left her feeling empty inside—burying a box in the brush, gathering rare herbs along a precarious cliff, reciting exotic words over the buried box—each task more unusual than the last. On the day they found her, she had been told to light the candle in the town center and guard it until sunrise to be free. She was sent home to her husband and child to recover.

"The villagers, suspecting dark magic, dragged Isobel into the church. She stood before a jury of men and was accused of bewitching the woman. But before she could be found guilty, the mother burst in, claiming she made it up to frame Isobel because she herself was consorting with the devil. Rumors say she began speaking that alien language again, her body crawling crab-like between the pews. Isobel was freed, but the mother of the boy... her fate was much worse."

A chill ran down my spine as we climbed back into the cart and Mr. Beaton cracked the reins and steered us back onto the road.

"That happened again and again, four times in total. Women were found in curious circumstances, their eyes erratic and bulging. Each one swore that Isobel was the culprit, only to later confess to witchcraft themselves. The last one was the minister's wife. When she was found, her nightgown was torn, her hair disheveled, and she clutched a black candle. She raved about Isobel, accusing her of dark deeds. But then, like the others, she broke down and admitted that it was her who was guilty. The whole village heaved with suspicion. Whispers of Isobel's true nature spread like wildfire. There was something off about her, they said. Something unnatural. But with no solid evidence against her, and confessions from the other women, they had to release her. Isobel didn't wait for the villagers to change their minds. After the burning of the minister's wife she vanished, slipping away under the cover of darkness and disappearing forever." He hesitated. "Well, that's not entirely true; there've been a few sightings of her passing through over the years, but I say that's phooey—just people trying to drag up the past." He flicked his wrist, brushing off the stories.

My stomach ached as it somersaulted under my skin.

"That's... quite the story..." I said. "But what... what about young Angus?"

Mr. Beaton sighed deeply. "Truth be told, we didn't know there was a young Angus until after Isobel disappeared. About a year after the event some local children, looking for a scare, went out to Isobel's abandoned home at the edge of town. There, they found young Angus inside." He scratched at his chin and stared into the distance. "Children can be cruel, Lilian," he said. "They tied a rope around her neck and led her barefoot into town, thwapping the back of her legs with willows the whole way. They gathered the townsfolk and claimed they'd caught a young witch in Isobel's cabin. I was there that day. She was bony and frail, and her eyes were wide with fear. She had this great mass of flaming red hair that was tangled like a bird's nest at the back of her head. The villagers were right riled up, convinced the children had brought more wickedness into our community. They were scolded for going to Isobel's home, and then young Angus was taken to the church too. She never admitted to knowing Isobel, she said she was orphaned and had found the cottage abandoned. She had hidden out in the garden for days, and when nobody returned, she went into the house. She'd been out there alone for months. Even the villagers couldn't help but feel sorry for her. The women gave her a bath and a clean frock, and she was allowed to stay in the old house.

"She spent a lot of time in the village at first, learning how to grow vegetables and cook from the women, but over time she began growing her own food and her visits became less and less. Angus proved to be a gifted midwife as well and began helping local women in exchange for small favors in return, but nobody thought anything of it because it wasn't to the extent of Isobel. Until a rich townswoman was struggling to birth her son. That was the day everything changed for Angus. The woman had labored for a full day and was growing weak. The other women were at their wits' end with what to do, so they decided to call on Angus for help. Angus did what she could, but the mother died, and the wee one too. Angus seemed to change after that. She pestered the grieving father for payment and threatened his other children if he didn't comply. That set off the chain of rumors that maybe she was like Isobel—or worse, Isobel's daughter. Eventually, Angus fled too. The cottage got boarded up and it's off-limits to all residents. Cursed, I tell ya, that place is cursed."

I hesitated before asking, "What do you think happened with Isobel and Angus?"

Mr. Beaton's face darkened, his eyes clouding over. "Well... I try not to dwell on it, Lilian," he murmured, his voice thick with unease. "But I don't believe their souls were good. Iona—she was good to her core, a bright spot in this dark world. But Isobel... and Angus." He faltered. "If anyone made a deal with the devil, well, it may very well be them."

The road to Edinburgh had been long and arduous, winding through rolling hills dotted with sheep, and crossing narrow rivers. The bumps of the rutted road rattled our aching bones.

I shifted back and forth in my seat trying to cure the numbness that had settled into my bottom.

"How much longer," I winced.

"Not far now," said Mr. Beaton through clattering teeth as he pointed to the horizon.

The city gates rose before us, and as we drew nearer, the air thickened with the stale smell of smoke, roasting meat, waste, and unwashed bodies. The stench was so strong, even from a distance, that enormous drops of water began to seep from my eyes. I pinched my fingers over my nose, and Mr. Beaton gave a soft chuckle.

"It's not going to get any better, lass. Ya may as well get used to it."

It was the noise that hit me next—a stark contrast from the quiet countryside. The city heaved under the cacophony of merchants shouting their wares and the clatter of wooden cartwheels on cobblestone; in the distance, bells rang out in deafening thongs.

Our cart rolled to a jerking halt at the gates, and I craned my neck to try and see what the holdup was. A man with a few cows pulled pointlessly on the neck of a heifer that laid itself down in the middle of the pathway. The other travelers hurled reprimands at him as he grabbed a great stick and began paddling the cow's rear end.

"God damn idiot," muttered Mr. Beaton, joining in the jeering.

I smirked—a medieval traffic jam.

Once the man finally removed his rogue cattle, crossing through the gate was a breeze. After years of siege, I expected something similar to a modern-day security check, but we simply plowed through and trotted our way into the city.

The winding streets teemed with people. Though the population of Edinburgh was small by modern day standards, it felt crowded and suffocating. The streets were a mishmash of classes: noblemen in rich cloaks, peasants in hand-spun garments, and feral children weaving their way between all of them. I looked skyward—the buildings, comprised of timber and stone, rose high on either side, their upper stories jutting out like broken bones.

I could see why Mr. Beaton brought his goods here. Market stalls lined the streets, brimming with produce, cloth, and trinkets. Merchants called out to passersby, and my ears were assaulted by the rowdy discussions of everything from gossip to the price of bread. On the horizon, hovering on top of a high hill, Edinburgh Castle rose—perched atop its rocky crag.

Mr. Beaton navigated through the masses with ease, yet I found myself gripping onto my seat, my knuckles turning white as I braced myself for a crash. As we neared Castle Hill, he pulled the reins to a stop outside a shabby inn. We crawled from the wagon, my legs still vibrating with phantom bumps as Mr. Beaton handed his reins off to a stable boy.

"Shall we?" he asked, gesturing to the door.

I stayed close to his heels as we entered the inn, squinting to adjust my vision to the smoky gloom. The air inside was suffocating, a blend of stale liquor and the earthy tang of peat fires. Laughter and lively conversation filled the space, punctuated by the occasional clink of tankards and the scrape of chairs on the rough wooden floor.

The inn was a modest establishment, its low ceiling supported by heavy beams, interspersed with stone. Flickering candles and oil lamps cast a warm, golden glow, creating pockets of light amidst the dimness. In one corner, a fiddler played a lively tune, his foot tapping rhythmically on the floorboards. A few patrons clapped along, their faces flushed with drink and heat from the large open hearth whose flame danced over a cast iron pot of stew.

Mr. Beaton led me to an empty table near the fire, and we settled on the sturdy, though slightly uneven, benches. A serving maid with rosy cheeks and a toothy smile approached, wiping her hands on her apron.

"What'll it be, then?" she asked, her voice carrying over the din.

"Ale for me and some bread and cheese," Mr. Beaton replied, glancing at his companion. "And for the young man?"

"I'll have the same," I said, deepening my voice midsentence. After my time on the journey and the truths that I told, I almost forgot about Jasper, the persona I was playing. Mr. Beaton winked at me.

"Right, lad. Almost lost it there, didn't ya."

Our food and ale showed up within minutes, and I took a sip of the amber liquid, savoring the rich flavor.

"Hmm," I murmured as I bit into the crusty bread. "I didn't realize how hungry I was."

Mr. Beaton chuckled, his eyes crinkling with amusement. "Well, it's been a long journey," he said, taking a hearty sip of his ale. "I've got an agreement with the innkeeper here—they always hold a room for me. You can share it if you don't have other arrangements. We can start fresh in the morning and figure out where they might have taken Iona."

His offer surprised me, the unexpected kindness warming me almost as much as the fire. I didn't deserve his kindness, but I was grateful for it. Truth be told, I had no plan. I had promised Mrs. MacCaffery that I would find Iona and free her, but uncertainty had been brewing inside me since our arrival at the gates. The bustling city stretched before me, and I had no idea where to start. Though I had been to Edinburgh many times in my own time, the city looked entirely foreign now. While the monumental features of Edinburgh Castle at the top and Holyrood Palace at the bottom of the sloped main street remained the same, everything in between had shifted.

As if reading my mind, Mr. Beaton interjected.

"We'll start at the markets in the morning," he began, his voice low. "It's the heart of the city, and word travels fast among the vendors. Someone might have seen or heard something about Iona."

I nodded. Even in modern times, markets were always bustling, a hub of activity where secrets were circulated as easily as prices.

"From there, we'll visit the inns and taverns," Mr. Beaton continued. "Travelers come and go, and innkeepers hear all sorts of stories. We'll ask discreetly—don't want to raise too much suspicion." His eyes met mine, conveying the gravity of our mission. "We need to be careful. Edinburgh isn't kind to those accused of witchcraft, and people might be wary of speaking out. But there are always those willing to talk for the right price or favor."

I swallowed hard. "What if no one wants to help us?" I asked.

Mr. Beaton smiled, a glimmer of determination in his eyes. "Then we'll look elsewhere. There are clandestine corners in this city—places where the outcasts gather. We'll find them. And if we have to, we'll search every nook and cranny of this place."

I nodded again in agreement. Mr. Beaton's plan was solid, and his confidence gave me strength.

"And remember," he added, his voice dropping to a near whisper, "trust no one but each other."

As the night wore on, the fiddler's tune slowed, and the chatter softened to a murmur, Mr. Beaton released a gigantic yawn, and my body involuntarily responded with one of my own.

"Time to retire," he said, and I nodded.

Mr. Beaton paid our barmaid, then he guided me up the stairs.

"Thank you for paying. I haven't much in the way of money," I confessed, for the first time aware of how ill-prepared I was. It was unlike me to be ill-prepared for anything, yet in this place and time, I seemed to be doing a lot of things "unlike me."

"Not a worry, lass," he said, shouldering the door to our quarters open.

The room was quaint, with a ceiling sloped unevenly toward the street below. Two simple beds, little more than hand-carved frames with straw-filled mattresses, stood against opposite walls. Each one was covered with a woolen blanket, stubbly to the touch but warm enough for the chilly Edinburgh nights.

I sat on the bed nearest to the door, the straw rustling under my body. Mr. Beaton moved to the window and peeked through the shutters to survey the street below.

"It's not much," he said, turning back to me with a reassuring smile. "But it's secure, and it'll do for the night."

I nodded, glad for the relative comfort as exhaustion enveloped me. I fell into a catatonic slumber replaying the plan in my mind—markets, the inns, the hidden corners of the city. It was a daunting approach, but I knew we had no choice. We had to find Iona and clear her name, no matter what it took.

Chapter Twenty-One

Morning arrived with the first light filtering through the small window, casting an artful radiance over the modest room. Mr. Beaton was already awake, sitting at the foot of his bed with his hands folded neatly in his lap, eyes bright and alert.

"Ah!" he exclaimed, spotting me stir. "You're awake and just in time. The city is waking as we speak. Let's go find Iona," he said, fidgeting with excitement.

I hesitated, then sat up, meeting his eager gaze. "About that, Mr. Beaton," I began, "you've done more than enough already. This could become very unsafe and I'm grateful for your kindness, but you came here to work. I'm taking up far too much of your time and resources"

Mr. Beaton sighed, a wistful smile crossing his face. "Lass," he said, taking a seat on the edge of his bed, "I've been alone for many years since Maeve passed, going through the motions and feeling quite lonesome. This may indeed be hazardous, but for the first time, I feel I have a purpose. And that purpose is to help you."

He paused, his eyes reflecting a lifetime of memories. "I know it might not be fun dragging an old man along on this search, but it would mean a lot to me to have one last big adventure before my bones are too old to carry me out the door."

I swallowed hard and crossed the room, taking a seat beside him and reaching out to clasp his hand. "Then let's find Iona together," I said.

Mr. Beaton's face broke into a broad smile, and his feet tip-tapped on the floor. "Thank you lass, you won't be disappointed."

We secured a few chunks of bread and cheese on the way out the door, and Mr. Beaton swallowed down a large mug of ale too. I politely declined the early morning brew, my stomach still unsettled from last night's meal.

"Grassmarket first," he said between chews of the sour bread as he marched straight and strong into the streets.

I kept close to Mr. Beaton—too close, really. A few times he turned to stare at me as my toes got caught in the back of his shoes, but even when he stumbled, he never got angry.

"It'll be okay," he said. "No need to be afraid." I nodded, thankful for his words. The Grassmarket felt like a labyrinth, each turn and alleyway revealing new sights and sounds, my senses overwhelmed by the chaos of the city.

"This is a good place to start," he said, halting at a small shop selling candles and charms. The proprietor was an elderly man with a keen smile and shifty eyes. He nodded as he listened to Mr. Beaton's description of Iona, promising to keep an ear out for any news, then directed us onward to an herbalist.

"If anyone knows, it'd be her," he said, pointing along the narrow, stall-lined path, his optimism unwavering.

We pushed through the throngs in the direction the man had sent us, pausing along the way for Mr. Beaton to greet other shopkeepers he knew. He was quite popular in this part of the world. After a lot of shoving and the seizure of one small boy by the collar of his shirt for the safe return of the coins he had pinched from Mr. Beaton's pocket, we arrived at the herbalist's booth.

Mr. Beaton leaned over her display, which was overflowing with vials and rank smelling salves, and whispered something in her ear. She cupped her hand and learned in to amplify his voice over the throngs of people. She pulled back and gave him a wary look that softened into a smile as he slipped a few coins into her open palm.

Her eyes darted around the stalls before she leaned forward and whispered something back.

Mr. Beaton nodded and reappeared at my side. He grabbed my elbow and steered me down a claustrophobic close.

"There are a few women who have been brought in from the villages on the accusation of witchcraft," he said, his lips pursed together as he rubbed his temple. "She didn't see them, but rumor has it they are being held at the castle mound. Five in total, all from villages outside of Edinburgh."

A shudder ripped through me at the thought of poor Iona trapped in that imposing place. "How do we get in?" I asked, glancing up at the vast fortress.

Mr. Beaton shook his head. "We don't. The castle is too heavily guarded. They don't let just anyone through those gates, especially not to see prisoners. The guards are strict, and the defenses are high. We wouldn't stand a chance of getting in and back out alive."

My spirits plummeted, as did my posture.

"But," he continued, "we can attend the trial. Trials for witchcraft are public and meant to be seen by the townsfolk. A bit of a scare tactic to dissuade people from participating in devil work. They hold them in the Great Hall of the castle. If Iona is to stand trial, we'll be able to be there, to see her and hear the charges against her."

"When?" I asked.

"Tomorrow, after sunset," Mr. Beaton said. My shoulders sank further downward as the hours between now and then flooded my mind. "But until then, we shall have a grand time in Auld Reekie." Mr. Beaton's eyes twinkled as he gave my shoulders a gentle squeeze, pulling them upward into a neutral position. I had been hugged more in the past two weeks than I had ever been in my entire life—and for some reason, I was starting to like it.

"Okay," I said, linking my arm through his. "Show me the sights of the city."

Chapter Twenty-Two

The sun hung high in the sky as we departed the bustling Grassmarket.

The cobblestones beneath our feet were slick with rain and sticky with residue. The air reeked of urine as I glanced at the upper windows of the crooked buildings towering over us and stepped further into the street.

"Good idea, lass," Mr. Beaton said, tapping my hand. "You never know when the shit'll get the ole' heave-ho out the window."

We both laughed, but I quickly grimaced. In this time, it was common for human waste to be tossed out of windows, and I didn't want to be caught underneath it. The waste in the street was bad enough that it caked the soles of my shoes as I skidded my feet on the rough cobblestones, trying desperately but unsuccessfully to remove the gunk. The sticky residue clung to me, its odour attaching itself like a great stinky leech.

Mr. Beaton guided me through the narrow closes and passageways of the old city, his eyes twinkling with the enthusiasm of a seasoned city veteran. As we turned a corner, my body went rigid when I came face to face with a prostitute and a man indulging in her offerings, unabashed.

"This is... quite the place," I stammered, turning away and blushing.

"It's just this one section. Try not to look," he said, pulling my elbow down the steep steps. We emerged at the bottom of the close and popped onto another long street of merchants peddling their wares.

Throngs of people and lively chatter surrounded me. I laughed as Mr. Beaton exaggerated a bow to a group of noblewomen, tipping an invisible hat. They huddled together and moved past, eyeing my hunchbacked and toothless friend with suspicion.

We zigzagged through the crowds, drawn toward the growing sound of music. I stood on my tiptoes to see over the heads of those in front of me, searching for the source of the melody.

Ahead, colorful banners fluttered, and the joyful noise of fiddles and flutes danced on the wind.

People were dancing in the street, and Mr. Beaton extended his hand to me, bowing at the waist.

"I'm sorry, sir, I… I can't dance," I sputtered, suddenly hyper-aware of the grace of other women and my distinct lack thereof.

"Nonsense, my lass," he said, grabbing my hands and twirling me in wide circles.

I stumbled, laughing, my body uncoordinated but happy.

"Come on, feel the rhythm!" he encouraged, his own steps light and carefree.

"I'm trying!" I chuckled as the spinning world decreased my coordination further.

As I spun, my gaze caught sight of a tall man moving through the crowd, his arm around a striking redhead. His lips grazed her ear, purring words just for her.

My heart leapt. It looked like Edgar. Could it really be him?

I faltered in the dance, my laughter fading.

"Are you alright?" Mr. Beaton asked, his brow furrowing with concern.

"I... I think I saw Edgar," I admitted, my voice barely a whisper.

Mr. Beaton looked perplexed. "Who's Edgar, lass?"

I shook my head, suddenly aware of how little Mr. Beaton actually knew about me and my predicament.

"Edgar... Edgar was the friend that was with me at Iona's when I said the terrible things I did." I hugged myself in regret. "He's the one who told me just how poorly I had behaved... I never thought I would see him again."

"Where?" he asked, and I pointed in the direction they had gone.

Mr. Beaton gripped my arm and pulled me through the swarm of people, his pace quick and purposeful. We weaved through the bustling crowd, the murmur of voices and the press of bodies bearing down on me. Finally, a gap in the sea of faces appeared, giving us a clear view of the two figures ahead.

"That's him!" I said, extending my arm in the air, preparing to call out to him. Then he turned to the redheaded girl and ran the back of his hand over her forehead and down her cheek. She leaned into it, and my resolve faltered.

I doubled over, clutching my abdomen as a tsunami of sorrow swept through me. Mr. Beaton looked at me, his eyes filled with knowing, and he took my hand and steered me in the opposite direction.

I didn't know where the sadness came from—I should be happy that Edgar found some sort of company and happiness after what I had done. But the recollection of his hand, those hands I had thought about in a constant loop since he laced my dress, caressing another woman's face, left me feeling as though my spirit had been torn from my body. Everything ached, every piece of me ached in a way I had never felt before.

"Let's go, lass. Let's get you out of here."

We walked through the winding streets, the noise of the market replaced by the disassociated hum of my brain, until Mr. Beaton steered me into a secluded tavern tucked away from the main thoroughfare. Inside, the gentle gleam of light and the low murmur of patrons provided a much-needed respite from the chaos outside. We took a seat at a corner table, away from prying eyes and ears.

Mr. Beaton ordered a modest meal, and as we waited for it to arrive, I stared into nothingness, my mind consumed with the image of Edgar's hands.

Our meal arrived—a small portion of stew—and Mr. Beaton slid mine toward me. I stirred it around on my plate, but the thought of eating made sour saliva pool in my mouth. I put my head in my hands and began to sob.

Mr. Beaton dropped his spoon and reached out for my hand.

"You'll feel better if you tell me about it lass," he said, his voice brimming with kindness.

I took a deep breath, the words tumbling out in a rush. "We're friends... We were friends. But I lied to him, and when everything happened with Iona, well... he pointed out how different I am from others and how I can be selfish and unaware of how others are feeling. He said I was a bad friend, and maybe an even worse person. He said I'm pretentious, and I think he's right. I feel like I don't belong."

Mr. Beaton listened intently, his expression thoughtful. "Lilian, let me be clear about one thing: you are odd."

My sobs returned and ricocheted through my body in staggering waves.

"Wait, wait," he said, patting my hand. "I'm not done."

"You're odd, you're a bit rigid, you bristle when people touch, ya—but you're also so very bright." His eyes twinkled. "You believe in right and wrong, you care deeply about it, and you're not afraid to go to extreme lengths to correct the mistakes you have made."

I blinked, surprised at his words.

"But I often get it wrong. I mean, look what I did to Iona... and Edgar."

He cut me off. "We all get it wrong sometimes, lass. That's the nature of being human, and even with your... unique qualities, you are still human." He winked at me.

I pushed my stew around on my plate.

"Friends argue, they hurt each other, but true friends also forgive. When you find him again, I'm sure you'll see friendship can transcend."

He placed an arthritic finger under my chin and coaxed my gaze upward to meet his.

"Lilian," he began, his voice soft yet probing, "I would not be a good friend to you if I didn't point out what is obvious to me... I believe there's somethin' deeper at play with your feelings. I understand your fear of losing Edgar as a friend, but I can't help but wonder if it's a bit more than that. Think about that moment when you saw him with another woman—the ache that gripped you, the way it sent you spiraling into the backstairs corners of your own mind. That kind of pain isn't about mending a rift between friends. It's more profound, more intense. It's love, Lilian."

I thought back to all the things I adored about Edgar. His infectious laughter that could brighten any room, the way his eyes sparkled with mischief when he told a joke, the comforting warmth of his presence. He always seemed to know exactly what to say to lift my spirits, and his unwavering support had seen me through countless challenges.

But were these not the hallmarks of an abiding friendship? Or was there something more beneath the surface, something I had been too oblivious to acknowledge? My mind raced through moments we had shared—our long conversations that stretched into the night, the way his touch lingered a fraction longer than necessary, the flutter in my chest whenever he smiled at me.

As I reflected, a new awareness began to take shape. The ache I felt when I saw him with another woman wasn't out of a need to right the wrongs between us; it was a profound sense of loss, a dread that someone else could occupy the room in his heart that I desperately wished was mine.

Could Mr. Beaton be right? Had I been blind to my own feelings, hiding behind the guise of friendship to shield myself from the vulnerability of love? The thought was terrifying.

"Even if you're right, sir, you were there, you saw the same tenderness I did. I ruined everything."

Mr. Beaton leaned forward. "Lilian, sometimes things are not always as they appear. The other woman you saw Edgar with might not have been what you think. It could have been a friend, or even a stranger he was helping. We often jump to conclusions when our emotions are involved, but it's important to seek the truth before assuming the worst." He paused, letting his words sink in. "But even if she was someone Edgar is interested in, you have to understand that he can't be expected to wait around if he doesn't know how you feel. Edgar is not a mind reader. If you haven't communicated your feelings, he might not have any reason to believe there's something more between you.

"True love requires courage, Lilian. It means being vulnerable and honest about your emotions, even when it's frightening. If your feelings for Edgar run deeper than friendship, he deserves to know. Keeping it hidden only creates more confusion and pain for both of you." He leaned back. "Consider this," he said, stroking his great long beard, "if you were in Edgar's shoes, wouldn't you want clarity? If you cared deeply for someone, wouldn't you want to know where you stood with them? By not expressing your true feelings, you're not giving him the chance to make an informed choice. Life is too short for untold truths. If you care for Edgar as much as I believe you do, then it's time to take a leap of faith. Tell him how you feel. If he shares your feelings, it could open the door to something beautiful. And if he doesn't, at least you'll have the closure you need to move forward, rather than living in a state of uncertainty."

I turned my eyes back to my stew, dragging my spoon through the meaty gravy.

"So, Lilian, if you find that your feelings for Edgar can endure the storms and conflicts, if you can still see the goodness in him even when you're upset, then perhaps what you have is indeed something more profound than friendship. True love isn't about the absence of arguments; it's about the presence of a bond that remains unbroken through it all."

The buzz of the bar swirled around us, but in that moment, a sense of peace settled over me. Maybe, just maybe, things could be alright. If I ever saw him again.

"Thank you," I said.

Mr. Beaton smiled back, his eyes crinkling at the corners. "Now, shall we join the festivities? I believe there's a dance coming up that demands our attention."

Chapter Twenty-Three

We danced until our feet ached and then limped back to our lodgings, blisters forming on the soft skin of our heels.

As we collapsed on our beds, Mr. Beaton sniggered contentedly. "Well, lass, you've given an old man such a lovely adventure, and I thank you for it."

I sighed. "I am grateful to you, Mr. Beaton, for everything."

He rolled over and looked at me. "We have until sundown tomorrow, Lilian. I think we should try and find your friend."

"I don't know," I hesitated, my mind racing with conflicting thoughts. "I have a lot to think about."

Mr. Beaton nodded knowingly, and before he had finished the motion, his eyes shuttered shut and he drifted off, a smile still grazing his lips.

Sleep evaded me as I rotated like a pig on a spit, my thoughts flickering between saving Iona and Mr. Beaton's words. Edgar's face surfaced in my mind's eye, and a pang of loss hit me. Who was that redheaded woman? My soul ached. "Why are you like this?" I muttered, pulling the blankets over my head, wishing desperately for an escape from my own thoughts.

When Mr. Beaton stretched with the sunlight, I was still there, curled on my side, staring at him wide-eyed. He looked at me with concern. "You didn't sleep," he said.

I shook my head. He moved to my bedside, the hay mattress shifting under his added weight as he sat beside me and placed a gentle hand on my back.

"I know you're missing your friend, and I know you're worried about Iona, but you need to try and rest because we need that brain working at full capacity this evening," he said, tapping on my forehead.

He pulled the blankets around me and tucked them tightly around my frame before planting a tender peck on my cheek.

"I'm going to go try and peddle some wares. You rest; I'll bring you some food in a bit."

His tenderness was comforting and parental, something that I lacked from my own mother. I felt secure here with him in his care, and the tender affection of his touch lulled me into a deep and dreamless slumber.

The aroma of warm bread roused me, and my eyes fluttered open to find Mr. Beaton sitting beside me in a hard-backed chair, ankle resting on his knee, engrossed in a book.

"I've slept all day," I said, jolting upright.

"Aye," he responded without looking up from his book. "And you're lookin' much better for it." A cheeky grin spread across his face.

He placed a plate of bread and soft cheese on my lap. "Eat. Then we should head toward the castle. It's best to arrive early."

I ate with the ravenous appetite of a starved animal, and downed an entire mug of ale in record time before we headed out the door.

We exited the inn, the cool evening air brushing against our skin. My legs wobbled beneath me from the rapid consumption of alcohol, and I could feel the heat rising to my cheeks. Mr. Beaton extended an arm to steady me.

"You'll get used to the drink here lass—but it takes some time."

"I don't know sir, I don't think I'm cut out for Scottish drink," I said, teetering side to side.

The city was quieter now, the day's hurry-scurry giving way to the subdued pace of night. Spectators, drawn by the morbid fascination of the trial, were the only ones on the street, streaming in single file toward the castle gates, their faces a mix of curiosity and apprehension. Trials for witchcraft drew large crowds, and today was no exception. Murmurs and whispers rippled through the audience, each new piece of gossip adding to the tension that hung over the city.

As we neared the front of the line, Mr. Beaton turned to me, his expression resolute. "Remember, Lilian, we must stay vigilant. Listen carefully, watch closely, and be ready for anything."

The heavily armed guards were a sobering reminder of the fortress's impenetrability. They stood tall and stoic, their eyes scanning the crowd for any signs of trouble. I eyed their towering figures as we passed through the gates.

"Don't look at them," Mr. Beaton said from the corner of his mouth. "Eyes straight ahead, just follow the crowd."

I nodded in quiet understanding as we were swept inside the castle walls. The single file line spread out as we entered the inner courtyard, and people scrambled amongst the soldiers and officials, searching for their friends.

We joined the flow toward the Great Hall, whose doors were swung open welcoming the prying eyes of society. My jaw fell agape as we entered the hall, a magnificent chamber with high ceilings and tall windows that let in streams of moonlight. A raised platform at the far end of the room held a throne-like chair where the presiding judge would sit, flanked by clerks and guards.

Mr. Beaton and I found a spot near the back where we had a solid view of the proceedings. My heart thudded as we waited, the minutes dragging by with agonizing slowness.

"We don't have a plan," I blurted out, panic rising in my voice. The last twenty-four hours had been a blur, my mind consumed with only Edgar. In my distraction, I had completely neglected my promise to Mrs. MacCaffery to save Iona. "Mr. Beaton, I'm sorry. I was so consumed in my own little world that we didn't come up with a plan." I clenched my fists beside my head, the frustration of my consuming thoughts gnawing at me.

He turned to me and grabbed my hands, pulling them away from my temples and cradling them gently between both of his palms. "Lilian, I've had all day to think. During the trial, I'll create a diversion to draw the guards' attention. When I do, you must use the opportunity to sneak Iona out of the courtroom."

"That sounds very risky. What if something happens to you?"

He gave me a reassuring smile. "I've lived a long life, Lilian. If I can use it to save Iona, then it's a risk worth taking. You're younger, quicker—you have a better chance of getting her to safety."

My voice wavered, and I swallowed hard. "But I can't just leave you behind. You've been so kind, and I can't bear the thought of something happening to you because of me."

He dropped my hand and moved his to my shoulders. "Lilian, this is the best way. We can't both cause trouble or Iona is doomed. If I can buy you even a few moments, it could make all the difference. Promise me you'll take the chance if it comes."

Water pricked at my eyes, but I nodded, swallowing hard. "I promise. I'll do everything I can to get Iona out of there."

He squeezed my shoulder. "Good lass. Now, keep your wits about you. When the time comes, you'll know what to do."

Three loud thumps of wood on stone rang out through the chamber. The doors at the side of the hall swung open, and five women emerged from the bowels of the castle, each one flanked by two guards. The third woman in line was Iona, her hands bound with crude and cutting rope. She looked washed-out and battered, but her eyes held a fierce determination. I gasped aloud at the sight of her and beads of sweat began to form at my temples. I clenched my hands together to steady the shake.

Iona was led to a small wooden stool in the center of the hall, facing the judge's chair. The judge, a stern-looking man with angular cheekbones and tiny peering eyes, entered and took his seat, signaling the start of the trial.

"Bring forth Magdalene Mantieth," he boomed as a hush fell over the crowd.

The guards brought the first woman forward, a frail senior with paper-thin skin tinged with a deathly greyish hue. She stood, head bowed, with one bruised and swollen foot hovering off the ground as the clerk began reading the charges against her.

"You have been brought to the Court of the Judiciary to face the charges of devil worship and cursing. What have you to say for yourself."

"I've never done nothing of the sort sir," she whimpered.

A rippled of chatter poured from the crowd.

The clerk sneered and raised his hand for silence.

"Bring forth Bessie Watsonne," he said as the guards grabbed a mousy woman from the front of the room by the collar and brought her before the bench.

"Mrs. Watsonne, you are Mrs. Manteith's neighbor and the one who has brought forth these charges, what say you to prove that she has conspired with evil forces."

"We-well sir," stuttered the timid woman, wringing her hands. "I saw 'er with me own eyes I did, down by the village mill. She had heaps of stones and was walking in circles and tossing 'em over her shoulder. Then she took some water from the mill in a stone dish, took three sips and spat it back into the water. The next morning the mill stopped working and it hasn't been right since."

The front row erupted in fervent hatred. "I saw her in the woods baptizing a rabbit I did," yelled a pudgy man.

"She made my husband's wand stand upright and it never lay down. He died!" the woman next to him wailed.

I rolled my eyes and looked to Mr. Beaton, who shook his head in disbelief.

The accusations flew fast and furious with pointed fingers and bared teeth as the dejected woman stood trembling, trying to defend herself against the unrelenting tide of superstition.

"It's not true!" she cried. "I didn't do nothing of the kind." She turned to her neighbor. "I've been good to you Bessie, when your husband was ill, I was the only one who helped you care for him." Her pleading eyes searched her neighbors face, but Mrs. Watsonne turned away, unable to meet her eyes.

The judge's verdict was swift and merciless. "Quiet!" he roared, silencing the onslaught of accusations with a raised palm.

"Mrs. Magdalene Mantieth, you have been found guilty on the charges of devil worship, animal baptism, and cursing the town mill. For your unholy acts you shall be strangled by the neck and your body burned at the stake at the hanging grounds. May God forgive you your trespasses."

The old woman's face crumpled, and she fell to her knees.

Suddenly, a young woman forced her way to the front. "No! Please, she's innocent!" she cried, reaching out. "Mother!"

She lunged forward, her fingers barely grazing the tips of the old woman's wrist when the forceful grip of a guard yanked her backward. She clawed at the guard, her nails marring his cheek with a ghastly gouge. The guard let out a howl of rage and wiped the trickle of blood from his cheek. "Bitch," he roared as he unsheathed a small dagger from his side and mercilessly plunged it into the young woman's flank. As she collapsed to the floor, he kicked her hard in the ribs, and she flopped over lifeless. Old Mrs. Mantieth let out a guttural scream that echoed through the hall. She crawled across the floor, cradling the limp body of her daughter in her arms.

"Dear God, why?" she cried to the heavens before looking to the guard. "Curse you, you bastard!" she screamed. "Curse you and your entire family."

The room went silent—and then chaos erupted into a maelstrom of violence and disorder. The air grew thick with tension. Shouts, screams, and the clash of metal against metal raged through the air. People surged like a turbulent sea sweeping up everything in its path, bodies crashing against one another as the guards formed a line, shields up and weapons ready to stem the tide of fury.

The noise was overwhelming, a constant barrage of sound that made it hard to think. The ground shook underfoot as more people joined the fray, their voices merging into a singular, thunderous roar. Adrenaline coursed through my veins as I searched the crowd for Iona.

"Guess I won't need to be the distraction," Mr. Beaton said as he grabbed hold of my wrist and steered me along the parameter of the mob.

"She's there," he said, pointing to the outskirts of the crowd. Iona had escaped the throng and was standing frozen, watching the chaos with her back pinned to the wall.

"Now, Lilian! Go!"

We pushed through the throng of people toward Iona, the press of bodies both a hindrance and a shield.

"Hold on, Iona!" I called out, almost inaudible over the din.

We reached her and scanned for guards before untying the ropes binding her wrists. "We need to go!" Mr. Beaton urged, aiming a wary eye at the armed men struggling to regain control. He seized Iona with one hand, and me with the other as he began weaving his way through the crowd, his years of navigating the streets of Edinburgh paying off as he crisscrossed through the throngs toward the door.

The exit was now in our sights. The cold air seeping in smelled of freedom, and we quickened our pace, throwing fleeting glances over our shoulders to ensure we weren't being followed. As we reached the exit, a hand clasped over my wrist, yanking me from Mr. Beaton's grip. I had been apprehended—we were all doomed.

"Go!" I yelled to Mr. Beaton. "I'll find you, just go!"

I turned to face my fate and my face crumpled.

There he was. Edgar.

"I knew it was you," Edgar said, choking down a lump in his throat.

Time froze as our eyes met, I wanted to hug him, shout at him, kiss him, and demand answers all at once. My legs felt like they were made of lead.

For a moment, everything else faded away. It was just the two of us in the midst of the chaos. But then I saw the guard standing a few feet behind Edgar, his eyes combing the crowd with the precision of a searchlight. Panic seized me, and all my conflicting emotions coalesced into one urgent thought: *Run!*

"We have to go!" I yelled as our fingers entwined, and we plunged into the crowd making for the exit.

We burst through the doors into the cold night, our legs and arms pumping in unison as we fled the castle. The air stung my lungs, and the sound of our footsteps echoed off the stone walls. Ahead, I spotted Mr. Beaton, his limp pronounced, with Iona struggling to keep up. We followed him down a steep set of steps in a dimly lit close. The cobblestones were slick underfoot, and the distant clamor of the castle faded as we found refuge in the darkness, chests heaving from the exertion and the adrenaline coursing through our veins.

Iona leaned against the wall, tears streaming down her face in an amalgamation of fear and relief. Edgar and Mr. Beaton stood beside her, their cheeks flushed from the exertion.

I approached Iona and clasped her face between my palms. "Iona I am so sorry, I never meant for this to happen to you. Please forgive me" I said. There was no response.

"You did it," I said, turning to Mr. Beaton. "You got her out."

He nodded, a weary but triumphant smile on his face. "Aye, lass. But we're not free yet. We need to get as far away from here as possible before they realize she's gone."

"I know a place," said Edgar. "Let's go."

Chapter Twenty-Four

Edgar

The night closed around us as we moved toward the safe house. The side streets of Edinburgh were silent, the riot's chaos now an unpleasant memory. Lilian and I walked ahead, our footsteps echoing off the cobblestones, while Mr. Beaton tailed behind holding Iona's hand.

The tension between us was thick. Having Lilian close again brought relief, but the memory of our argument weighed heavily on my chest. Each step felt like a tightrope walk where one misstep could either bring us closer or reignite the fight.

I stole glances at her side profile, searching for any sign of how she was feeling, but her expression was guarded. The familiar comfort of her nearness felt tainted by harsh words and hurt feelings. My mind raced, replaying the argument, wondering if there was a right moment to address it, to say something that might bridge the gap.

I opened my mouth to speak, to apologize, to explain, but no words came. Instead, I concentrated on the rhythm of our footsteps, hoping the shared movement might somehow ease the tension.

The moon hung high in the sky, diffusing a soft, silvery glow over the world. I stole one more look at Lilian.

She was bathed in an ethereal light that highlighted the fine chiseled details of her face and the subtle waves of her hair. Despite her attempt at concealing herself as a boy, she looked breathtakingly beautiful, a serene presence amidst the chaos. It gave me the tenacity I needed.

"Lilian," I said, breaking the silence.

She turned her face toward me, her brows furrowed slightly, a question in her eyes. I took a deep breath.

"I… I need to say something, and I need you to hear me out."

She nodded, curiosity and caution dancing over her face, but continued to move forward.

"You look so beautiful tonight," I blurted.

Lilian's cheeks flushed, and she turned her face further away, unsure of how to respond. I cringed—that's not how I wanted to start—but it was out there and there was no way to take it back, so I pushed forward.

"I don't think you realize how beautiful you are. The way the moonlight touches your skin... it's like you're glowing. I've always thought you were beautiful, but tonight... tonight, you look like an angel."

Silence.

"But it's not only your appearance, Lilian," I stammered, my words quickening as they spewed forth. "It's who you are. You're good and pure, in a way that I've always admired. You have this light inside you, this kindness and strength that I can't even begin to describe. And I... I messed up." I sighed, running a hand through my hair. "I messed up so badly, Lilian. I can't believe the things I said to you." My voice trembled. "I hurt you and pushed you away when all I wanted was to be close to you. I was scared. I know it's not an excuse, but I was scared of not being good enough. What you said about Lizzy, about how she made you feel, it crushed me because all this time I've been trying to show you how much I adore you. I know things haven't been easy for you and I promised myself that I would make your future brighter. When you told me how you felt—how Lizzy made you feel, I realized I had failed to show you how wonderful you are." I looked down, my hands shaking. "You are wonderful you know."

Lilian softened, and she opened her mouth to interject.

I held up my hand. "I am not trying to interrupt you, but I have to ask that you please... let me finish. If I don't get this out, I may never find the courage again to say it. I know I don't deserve your forgiveness." My voice cracked. "But I need you to know how sorry I am. You mean everything to me, Lilian. I've been such an idiot and I can't stand the thought of losing you because of my cruelty."

Lilian's eyes shimmered as she reached out and gave my arm a gentle squeeze.

"Edgar," she began. I tensed, anticipating her response. I had never addressed her so bluntly before, but the uncertainty of the past few days had surged through me, spilling out in an uncontrollable torrent of emotion. "Sweet Edgar." She began shaking her head in disgust. My insides felt as if they were free-falling. "I don't think you're the one who should be apologizing."

The knot in my core began to loosen.

Her voice broke as she struggled to maintain her composure. "I'm so disappointed in myself for my behavior. You have been a constant in my life for five years now, an enduring voice of encouragement and support. You've always been there for me, lifting me up, believing in me when I couldn't believe in myself. And yet, I lied to you about Lizzy because I didn't want you to see how weak and insecure I really am, how badly I long for acceptance. You've done everything you could to help me, Edgar. You've embraced my awkward routines and my quirky personality with such compassion and kindness. You've never pressured me to be someone I'm not. I was blinded by my own self-hatred, and I couldn't see how good and kind you were to me. I couldn't see that you were always on my side, always rooting for me. And for that, I am sorry." Her breath shuddered in her chest as she struggled to find the courage to continue. "I saw you in the market, Edgar, with that beautiful redhead—I understand that this apology is likely coming too late. But please know, I will never take your friendship for granted again. I will be here for you in whatever capacity you would like me in your life, because I know now that my life is a lot less fulfilling without you near."

I stopped walking and turned to face her, my eyes swimming with curiosity.

"The redhead, where? When?"

Lilian stopped and a look of anger crossed her face.

"Oh, come on, Edgar..." she began, but I interjected with a laugh, covering my face in my hands.

"Oh my god, of course... the market!" I said, drawing closer and stealing a peek over my shoulder at Iona and Mr. Beaton, who were eyeing us with curiosity. "Lilian, that is Angus. Gelis and I found her not long after arriving in the city. We've been staying with her on the edge of the city—that is where we are headed now."

"Ah," said Lilian coldly. "I see she's just as beautiful as Iona said—you two seem to be getting along swimmingly."

Did I detect a note of jealousy? My heart flipped over in my chest at the thought.

"Lilian, while I understand that you take things at face value, let me assure you I was only checking to see if she was okay. She has been burning up with fever the past few days, so Gelis sent me to the market with her to see a healer. The healer gave us some herbs and we were heading back to her accommodation when she grew woozy. I was making sure she got there safely."

"Ha! Told ya!" Mr. Beaton responded from behind, and Lilian shot him a corrosive glare.

A tear slipped down her cheek and she wiped it away, aggressively turning her face from me.

"I'm such an idiot" she began.

I reached out and placed my hand under her chin, drawing her gaze back to me. Her eyes searched mine as I gently wiped the tear away.

"Lilian, you are not an idiot. I'm here, and I always will be. We'll get through this together. We have both made mistakes, but a wise man once told me, friends argue, they hurt each other, but true friends also forgive."

Lilian's eyes widened and she shot a second discerning look at Mr. Beaton, who curled his lip into a pout and shrugged, a twinkle glistening in his eye.

I took Lilian's hand and brought it to my lips, placing a whisper of a kiss on her knuckles. A tiny gasp escaped her lips.

"I am so thankful you are ok. I couldn't imagine a world without you in it."

She covered her eyes with her free hand and turned from me like a giddy schoolgirl.

"Ooooh," came a tease from behind us. We turned to see Mr. Beaton and Iona beaming in our direction.

"Glad to see you two friends are on good terms again," Mr. Beaton winked.

"This is your doing, isn't it? You're the reason Edgar was at the trial," Lilian said over her shoulder.

"Well, I couldn't let the two of you miss the chance at making things right."

I turned to Lilian. "He found me near the market yesterday afternoon—said that I may see someone at the trial I'd been longing to see. He was right, you know. I've missed you terribly." I gripped her soft hand tighter, then looked to Mr. Beaton. "Thank you, sir."

"Aye, lad, happy to be of assistance," he said, bowing gently.

"So where did you two cross paths?" I asked them both as we walked on, the tension from earlier evaporating.

Lilian took a long breath. "After you left, I went back to the village to learn more about Iona. In a tavern, I overheard some drunkards talking about how she was being held in the church. They said awful things, Edgar. I knew I had to act."

My eyes widened with concern.

"I went to the church, determined to save her. When I got there, I found Mrs. MacCaffery—you know, the pregnant woman from that day." Her voice shuddered as she recalled Iona's cottage. "Her husband was the one torturing Iona. I don't think he had stopped beating her since we fled."

I placed a hand on Lilian's arm. "What happened then?"

"Mrs. MacCaffery told me they planned to take Iona to the Capital for trial, but we couldn't intervene there. Her husband was like a rabid dog—he would have killed us both on the spot. Knowing I couldn't make it on foot, she introduced me to Mr. Beaton, who does business here," she said, gesturing behind her. "On the journey, he told me he heard me in the pub and knew I wasn't who I said I was, so I told him the truth." Her voice lowered to a whisper. "Well, except for the time travel part. Iona had helped his wife Maeve in the past, and when he learned I wanted to help her, he insisted on coming along."

"So, that's how you came together."

Lilian nodded. "Yes. He knew the risks, but he wanted to repay Iona for her kindness, and has since done so much more for me than that."

I looked over at the slumped but brave old man who walked quietly with Iona, gentle and protective. "Mr. Beaton," I said softly, "thank you for everything you've done, thank you for protecting my friend. Thank you for finding me and bringing me to her—I left her behind, I never should have, and I promise you I won't again. Thank you for your bravery. I owe you, sir."

Mr. Beaton looked up, surprised by the heartfelt thanks. "It was the least I could do, son. We all have to stand up for what's right."

We walked together, the four of us, the city fading into the backdrop as the buildings spread further apart.

Chapter Twenty-Five

The safe house lay at the end of a dilapidated row of houses. To an onlooker, it would appear uninhabitable, but it had become home to Angus—an outcast even in a city as weird and wonderful as Edinburgh. I approached the entrance and knocked rapidly twice, paused, and added one more small knock—the signal that it was me and not an intruder or someone looking for trouble. I pushed open the door and peeked inside. The front room was dark and thick with the aroma of mildew. I swept the door open and moved to the side. "Come in, quickly," I said, ushering the group through the door.

Inside, the twilight glow revealed worn, dusty furniture shrouded in sheets and creaking floorboards that squealed with every step. Mr. Beaton hobbled forward and dragged a chair from the table in the front room. He held both of Iona's hands and lowered her frail body, trembling with exhaustion, into the seat. He then shuffled to a small table scattered with dishes and food scraps and searched for a mug. "There we go," he muttered under his breath as he found a cup, blew the dust out of it, and dunked it into a bucket of drinking water. He moved back to Iona, knelt in front of her and held the cup to her lips. "You must drink," he encouraged, worry casting great crevasses in his already wrinkled face.

I glanced at Lilian. "I'll go find Gelis. She's going to be thrilled to see you." Her eyes met mine and her lashes fluttered, causing my stomach to flip. I moved to the back of the tiny room to the only other door in the space and knocked. "Gelis," I called out, "she's here."

"I'll be there in a moment, just changing the sheets," Gelis called back.

I returned to Lilian's side. She was kneeling beside Mr. Beaton, who was wiping Iona's brow with a damp cloth he had produced from his pocket. "Thank you again for everything," she said, her tone soft and airy—very un-Lilian like. "Your bravery and kindness mean more than I can say."

Mr. Beaton looked up, his features drawn and dull. "It's what had to be done, lass."

"I wish I could have met Maeve," Lilian continued. "She was lucky to have such a brave and loving husband."

Mr. Beaton's eyes glistened. "She was the light of my life," he said. "And now, helping you and Iona... it feels like I'm honoring her memory."

The door creaked open and Gelis appeared, her face lined with concern. Lilian rushed forward and, without her usual hesitation, wrapped Gelis in a warm hug. "Gelis, thank goodness you're here," she exclaimed, her voice tinged with relief. Gelis beamed with surprise at the unusual display of affection, but as she looked over Lilian's shoulder and spotted Mr. Beaton, her expression darkened.

Mr. Beaton raised his head and met Gelis's eyes. He dropped his cloth to the floor, shot to his feet, and yanked Lilian from her arms.

"Get away from her!" he shouted, pushing Lilian behind him.

"What are you doing sir?" Lilian asked, trying to pull herself from his grip. "This is our friend Gelis, the one who was with us at Iona's."

Gelis released a low, menacing chuckle that made the tiny hairs on my arms stand on end.

"It can't be, lass," Mr. Beaton said, shaking his head back and forth. "That's Isobel, I'm sure of it." He hissed, "That's the one I was telling you about."

Lilian shook her head. "It's not possible Mr. Beaton, Gelis found us and has been helping us on this journey, she is good and kind."

The kindness Lilian praised disappeared from Gelis's features in a flash as she sauntered toward Mr. Beaton. "Well, well, well," she hissed. "I never expected to see you here."

Angus emerged from the depths of the darkened room, her expression wicked, with no signs of illness. She scanned the space with a predatory gaze, a cruel smile twisting her lips. "Hello, Mr. Beaton, thought I recognized your voice," she sneered, "and Lilian Darling, I assume?"

"And Angus too..." uttered Mr. Beaton. "I never thought I'd see the day when you'd show your faces together. You've brought nothing but suffering and despair to our people with your vile acts."

Isobel smirked, a glint of malice in her eyes. "Oh, Mr. Beaton, always so righteous. You can't possibly understand the reasons behind our actions."

Angus chuckled darkly. "Your precious village was a playground for us, a means to an end, if you will." She paced the floor like a rabid dog.

Mr. Beaton's fists clenched at his sides, his knuckles turning white. "So, it's true, you are both rotten to the core, and to think I believed that there might actually be good in your souls."

Angus stomped across the floor, her arms swinging at her side. "You should be more concerned about your own soul than ours, Mr. Beaton. Your suffering will be a lesson to all who dare oppose us." She moved like a striking snake, her arm a swift blur as she seized Mr. Beaton, twisting his frail arms behind his back and pinning him against her. He winced in pain.

"No!" Lilian screamed, lunging for him as Iona leaped to her feet, brandished a rusty knife, and pressed the blade against Lilian's throat, the metal biting into her skin.

"Ah, ah Lilian," she cackled, "we can't have any of that. You stay right here."

"Iona? What are you doing! Mr. Beaton and I saved you!" Lilian choked as she tried to pry Iona's hand from her neck.

"Saved me? You put me into that mess in the first place," Iona sneered. "Your weak attempt at an apology doesn't warrant forgiveness. I suggest you don't fight, I'm still pretty angry at you for messing up the plan."

"What do you mean the plan?" I snapped as I stepped towards Lilian. Iona dug the blade deeper into her skin, and she winced as the blade nicked the skin sending a small trickle of blood slithering down the length of her neck.

"Don't think I won't kill her," Iona warned, though her voice lacked conviction. I raised my arms in the air in surrender, turning to Gelis.

"Gelis?" I choked, my voice stinging with fear and confusion. "What the hell is going on! Help them!"

Gelis smiled coldly. "I suppose you deserve an explanation," she began, "but first, let me *re-introduce* myself." She bowed at the waist. "I am Gelis Isobel Alasdair Grey, head of the coven of Border witches, and these two lovely ladies are my coven sisters." She rose and gestured to Angus and Iona, who waved manically while still holding my friends captive.

The room seemed to press inward, shrinking around me as Gelis twisted the hem of her dress in her hands, marching around the room like an actor performing a soliloquy.

"I know this is a lot to absorb lad, and it's been a hell of a time keeping this secret from you, but there are things in this world your textbooks can't explain and we three are one of them." Her arms swept towards Angus and Iona. "Women, yes—but not mere mortals. Witches—but not your textbook definition. We exist across centuries, living for eternity. We shift through time and place, surviving in all millennia. The only way to rid the world of us is by turning our bodies to ash."

I stumbled backward and pressed my hand against the wall for balance.

"This is impossible," I whispered.

"Improbable yes, but I assure you it's possible. The three of us have existed together in many mortal lifetimes. We protect each other and work together, exchanging healing magic for favors that improved our living circumstances. In all other times we accomplished this with relative peace. But this time, this place in history, keeping our identities secret was much more challenging. Witches are real boy, and we are powerful, even more so together, but this place is unsafe and we learned that the hard way."

She was at the back of the room now, casually leaning on a window sill, wiping a small circle of grime away with her sleeve so she could peer outside.

"The first time we lived this life, we moved to Mr. Beaton's village and helped women in exchange for favors that advanced our plans. Wealth, security, beautiful gowns—you name it. In other lifetimes and timelines, the women would do our bidding and their behaviors would be chalked up to illness, but here, it became so much more. After that unfortunate incident in North Berwick, where a group of witches tried to intervene in mortal politics and turned the attention of the King to the existence of witches, things began to change. We met one evening and decided that in order to protect ourselves from similar outcomes we needed powerful magic. Young Angus here was charged with conducting a safety spell. She had one simple task: secure the blood of a pure spirit that would allow us to cloak our cottage in a peaceful serenity and shield us from the dangers outside. As luck would have it, a mother in the village was experiencing a difficult birth. The villagers called on Angus to assist."

"I told her I would do what I could to save the child, but the cost would be high. The cost would be the breath of his life. One vial of blood that contained the pureness of his humanity. He'd live but it would be a soulless existence. No joy, no love, just an unfeeling journey through actuality," cackled Angus.

Isobel shot her a frustrated look and Angus cowered like a beaten dog under her glare.

"I'm sorry Isobel," Angus whimpered.

"Shut it!" snipped Isobel, turning her gaze from the window and advancing on Angus. "Like she said, she had *one* job: capture the soul of the innocent child. But young Angus made a critical error, she misjudged the extent of a mother's love. The mother chose to end her life and the life of her child instead of condemning the wee one to a life without feeling. Angus tried to use our spellbook to capture the soul before it left this plane, but she was interrupted by the father, who seeing the book in her hand and his loved one's lifeless bodies on the bed, captured her and took her to the Capital for trial. Our book was used as evidence and then Angus was burned at the stake.

"Iona and I were left adrift in a sea of grief. Not only had we lost our friend, we lost the book that carried us safely through eternity. For safety's sake, Iona and I split up, and without our spell book or our coven, our lives seemed empty. Free from magic and friendship." Iona shifted uncomfortably from foot to foot. "I went to Iona once and said we should search for the book. The magic was strong enough that we could return to the past and save our friend. We would then flee Scotland together for a safer life somewhere else until the storms of trials and accusations blew over." Isobel faltered, her voice laden with centuries of grief. "But Iona's faith had waned."

Iona stuttered "I-I told Isobel I'm tired of hurting and hiding and that maybe we could actually use our powers for good."

Isobel's anger now turned to Iona.

"Yes. She left me alone to search for myself. I spent over 200 years hiding until the Witchcraft Act was repealed in the 1700s. I then rejoined society and scoured the countryside in search of our book so I could bring Angus back and restore our rightful place of power. I found nothing for hundreds of years, and then in 2010 I read an article about a young woman making strides in restoring the dignity of those who died in the witch trials. So I made my way to Oxford to see what she knew."

Lilian's jaw dropped as the realization washed over her.

"I knew you looked familiar," Lilian whispered in awe. "Lizzy?"

"Yes," Isobel interjected. "In your timeline, I existed as Lizzy, prowling the halls of that godforsaken university, trying to pry information and archival records from your stubborn hands.

When I became frustrated, you had to go all concerned about me and report me to the advisor. I went away, discouraged. Then just this year, I saw Angus's old house had sold. While my faith in recovering my lost friend had waned, I couldn't help but go look around. Then, I found that spell. I don't know how it got there—it seemed like a miracle, but it was the first evidence of the book I had seen for centuries. I reached out to you, hoping that the find would appeal to your insatiable desire to find answers. That it would spur your brain into overdrive in search of the artifact and as luck would have it, you creature of habit, it did. When we met at the Temple of the Muses and you handed me the book, I had everything to make things right. I began the spell under the ancient archways to move myself backward through time."

My face paled as the realization of their manipulation sank in. "And when Lilian and I latched onto you during the spell…"

"You were transported back through time with me," Isobel finished, her smile wicked and triumphant. "An unexpected twist, I will admit, but I cared not about what the future held for you in this world, I only cared about finding my friend. Except Lilian, always the disruptor, had to pry the book from me as the spell took hold, so I was still missing a critical piece of restoring our coven."

Lilian's eyes filled with tears of anger and betrayal. "Why didn't you just take the book when you found us in the cave, instead of pretending to be our friend?"

"Because you sleep like a duck Lilian, one eye open and half your brain always engaged. I realized that you could serve a greater purpose though. Taking you to Iona would show her that I had returned and that a shift had taken place that would allow us to save Angus. So I wrote her. I told her I had a surprise and to prepare some henbane tea. When I had proven to Iona that I had returned, we issued the potion, and when you were asleep, I took the book from the ripped hem of your dress. Truth be told the tea should have killed you. My coven-mates appear to be more incompetent than I remembered."

Iona dropped her eyes and cowered.

"You didn't expect me to accuse Iona of being a witch, did you?" Lilian inquired.

"No," Isobel admitted, her face darkening like a stormy sky. "That was unforeseen. It left us in the same position we were in before. So, I toyed with your fickle human emotions and encouraged you to save Iona. I brought Edgar with me to find Angus because he loves you too much to ever leave you, so I knew that the two of you would eventually be reunited and bring us back together."

I shook my head, disbelief and horror mixing in my eyes. My gaze darted to Lilian at the mention of love. She didn't seem to notice.

"So... you used us all along," whimpered Lilian.

Isobel's smile widened, cruel and triumphant. "Yes, and now with my friends back together and our book in our hands, we can complete the safety spell and live the rest of our lives in this timeline in peaceful protection. But there's still one missing piece—an innocent soul."

She moved with calculated grace toward Mr. Beaton, drawing a long, gleaming blade from the folds of her skirt. Without a moment's hesitation, she plunged the blade into his heart and dragged it downward.

A guttural wail tore from Lilian as she ripped herself from Iona's arms and rushed to Mr. Beaton. She caught his slumping body in her arms, his life slipping away. Blood oozed from the gaping wound, spreading across his shirt and staining Lilian's hands.

Mr. Beaton's eyes, wrought with pain and dismay, met Lilian's as his breathing grew shallow. Desperation etched deep lines into Lilian's face as she cradled him, her tears fused with the blood, creating crimson-streaked trails down her hands as she fumbled to close the wound.

Behind them, Angus knelt on the ground and gathered a small vial of blood from the growing pool on the floor.

Mr. Beaton's eyes fluttered, his breath coming in ragged gasps. He reached up weakly, his hand brushing against Lilian's tear-streaked cheek.

"Lilian," he whispered, his voice barely audible. "You have... a good heart... never forget that." His eyes searched hers, trying to convey a lifetime of wisdom in his final moments. "You've... given an old man... a grand adventure... for that, I... am contented."

Lilian clung to him, her fingers intertwining with his. "Please, Mr. Beaton, stay with me," she pleaded, her voice breaking.

The tension in his features eased, and the hard lines around his mouth relaxed. Despite the pain etched in his expression, he managed a faint smile. "My dear... you must be strong. Carry on... with kindness. Promise me... you'll... never give up... and don't forget... true love Lilian... that requires true courage."

Lilian choked, a storm of heartbreak consuming her as she felt his life slipping away.

His hand fell limp and a smile crept over his lips. "Hi Maeve... my darling," he gurgled. "I've missed you." And he took his final breath.

Lilian's sobs rattled the room as she held his lifeless body, the reality of his death crashing down around her. The burden of their mission, the grief of loss, and the anger at Isobel's cruelty all erupted in a volcano of emotion.

She looked up at Isobel her eyes alight. "You will pay for this," she vowed, her voice steady. "I will burn you myself for this."

"That's where you're wrong, lass," Isobel cackled, her voice dripping with malice. At that moment, Iona and Angus struck simultaneously, their blows landing with sickening force. Agony exploded in my head; the world tilted and swayed as I fell to my knees. I saw Lilian crumple beside me, her eyes agape with shock before everything faded to black.

Chapter Twenty-Six

I awoke on the cold, hard floor, my head throbbing and the rusty taste of blood in my mouth. My sense of time was rattled—minutes or hours may have passed, I couldn't tell. As my vision cleared, I saw Lilian slouching near Mr. Beaton's now rigid body, the fabrics of her outfit soaked in his blood. The air was thick with the sharp scent of iron and the haunting whisper of death.

Lilian's eyes fluttered open. Her face twisted with horror and grief. She scrambled across the floor, desperate to distance herself from Mr. Beaton's lifeless form. We were alone. Iona, Isobel, and Angus had vanished, leaving us with our throbbing heads and the corpse of our dear friend.

I crawled to Lilian; my own pain forgotten in the face of her anguish. I wrapped my arms around her and held her close as her sobs wracked her body. Childlike and crumpled, she buried herself in my shoulder as I murmured soothing words into her matted and bloody hair.

"It's going to be okay," I whispered, though I didn't know how. "We'll find a way through this. We'll stop them."

Lilian's sobs subsided and she clung to me. "We can't just let them leave," she said, her eyes burning with determination. "We need to find them. They need to pay…" She gulped, her gaze lingering on Mr. Beaton's lifeless body. "They need to pay for hurting him."

"I know," I said. "From what Isobel said, their magic must be done somewhere sacred—that's why she had us meet her at the Temple of the Muses. What is the most sacred ground near here?" I asked.

Lilian wiped her face with her hands, then seeing they were soaked in blood, stopped immediately. "The Kirkyard," she said.

I looked at her, puzzled.

"Greyfriars Kirkyard. It's still new-ish right now, but it is certainly sacred, and I imagine it's quiet this late at night." She rose to her feet and pulled a blanket from the small rocking chair in the corner. Draping it over Mr. Beaton, she whispered, "I will miss you, sir." With a final, sorrowful glance, she turned her back and strode out the front door.

I followed her, the weight of our mission an invisible anchor dragging us down. The night air was cold and still, punctuated only by distant sounds of civilization. We walked in silence, as we approached Greyfriars Kirkyard, the gravity of what lay ahead pressed down on us. We were stepping into the dangerous unknown, driven by our need for justice.

The entrance to the Kirkyard loomed before us, raising goosebumps on my arms. This was it—the place where we would confront Isobel and attempt to put an end to her vile plans.

Lilian halted at the gate and her eyes met mine. "Are you ready?" she asked.

I nodded, interlacing my fingers with hers. "Let's do this."

Greyfriars Kirkyard lay shrouded in eerie tranquility under the pale light of the moon. In this timeline, the Kirkyard was in its infancy. The weathered tombstones of the Greyfriars I had toured in modern Edinburgh now stood like glistening gemstones in the moonlight, their inscriptions legible, not yet worn and dulled by centuries of wind and rain. Tall, gnarled trees draped long silhouettes over the uneven ground, their branches dancing in the cool night breeze.

We moved with precision; our steps muffled by the moss underfoot. All was quiet, with only the distant hoot of an owl and the rustling of leaves breaking the silence. The outline of Greyfriars Church loomed against the night sky, its stone walls bathed in silver light.

Lilian moved ahead, her eyes darting across the darkened landscape. The dim shapes around us danced, shifting and flickering with life.

"There," Lilian gulped, pointing toward a secluded corner where the darkness was deepest. "That's where they'll be. It's the most secluded spot, ideal for their ritual."

We made our way toward the corner, our hearts pounding with anticipation. The air grew colder, and our breath began to appear as small white wisps with each rapid exhale. The gravestones leaned in, as if trying to warn us of the danger that lay ahead.

Lilian gripped my hand. "This is it," she said, jutting her jaw forward. "We stop them here."

She moved to step forward, but I gently pulled her back.

"Lilian," I whispered. She turned to me, her eyes wide and searching.

"What is it?" she asked.

I stuttered; my tongue heavy in my mouth. The words I had rehearsed a thousand times over the past week tangled together, refusing to leave my lips, but I forced them out, my voice quivering with wordless emotion. "Before we go in there, I need you to know something," I said, my voice barely above a whisper. "I love you, Lilian. I always have. Whatever happens tonight, I want you to remember that."

Her eyes widened in surprise, and for a moment, the world around us stood still. The cold night air, the rustle of leaves, and the faint murmurs of the witches all blended into an indistinct hum. Lilian's eyes softened and a flicker of emotion passed through them. She opened her mouth to speak, but no sound came out. Her jaw opened and closed, but no words escaped.

I watched her struggle, my heart sinking with each passing second. I had hoped for a different reaction, but as the silence stretched on, reality began to settle in.

Lilian finally managed to stammer, "Edgar, I... I don't know what to say."

Her eyes darted away. She swallowed hard, as if she were trying to choke down a piece of stale bread.

I nodded slowly, the acceptance of her inability to reciprocate dawning on me. I forced a smile, but it did not reach my eyes.

"It's okay, you don't have to say anything. I just needed you to know how I feel."

I moved back, creating a respectful distance between us, her quietness cutting through me like jagged shards of glass.

I was a fool for hoping that my feelings might be reciprocated.

"Let's get moving then," I said.

Lilian gave a small, determined nod, and cast one last, lingering look at me. "For Mr. Beaton," she said. She turned and marched toward where Isobel and her coven awaited, leaving me standing there, my heart in tatters.

LILIAN

H e loves me.

He stood there, eyes full of earnestness, pouring out his innermost feelings, and all I could do was flounder in place. My mind whirling.

Mr. Beaton was right—I love him too. At least, I think this is love. But for me, love is a tangled web. Is it simply wanting to be near someone, to relish their existence? Or is it that deep, aching thirst from romance novels? My chest tightened with the uncertainty. I craved to understand, but the terror of making a misstep paralyzed me.

The world I see is different from others. Desire doesn't sweep over me like a tidal wave, but I crave Edgar's company above all others. Most people irritate me; their presence overwhelms me with an insistent buzzing, demanding my attention, requiring me to play a role. My tranquil life unsettles them—they can't grasp it. But not Edgar. With him, everything shifted. He illuminated my life in ways I never anticipated, a constant warmth in my often-shadowed world.

I should have spoken. I should have stepped forward, wrapped my arms around him, kissed him with all the feelings churning inside me. Instead, I let the words fester in my mind: "I love you too, Edgar," I mouthed, hoping the mantra would summon the courage I was seeking.

If we survive this, I vow to tell him. I will find a way to voice the feelings I can barely comprehend but know exist.

But what if I fail him? What if my love isn't enough? What if my words fall flat, leaving him empty? The thought buried deep in the folds of my brain, refusing to give me peace.

I flicked my hands, trying to shake off my uncertainty. Now was not the time. Now I needed to focus. Now I needed to avenge Mr. Beaton's death. We had reached the clearing, and the women came into view. Rage coursed through me as I remembered Iona and Isobel and their deception. My hands shook in angry fists at my side.

In the secluded clearing, a faint glow flickered, flinging an eerie light over the surrounding tombstones. Silhouettes danced within the light, and the faint murmur of voices reached our ears. Isobel and her coven were here, preparing to complete their dark spell.

We took shelter behind a large oak tree, peeking around it, trying desperately to formulate a plan of action.

Isobel stood at the center, commanding and enigmatic. Her hair cascaded down her back in kinky waves. Her eyes, shifty and piercing, glowed with an unnatural light as she chanted in a primeval, forgotten language, her voice resonating with power.

To her right, Angus stood with a stoic expression, cradling the spellbook. Her voice joined Isobel's, adding a low, melodic harmony to the chant, her eyes fixed on the candle flickering between them.

On her left, Iona completed the trio, her vivid green eyes looking frightened and uncertain. Her voice, higher and more lyrical, wove through the other two, a less enthusiastic melody echoing through the graveyard.

The ground around them was marked with intricate symbols and runes, drawn in a mixture of salt and blood that shimmered in the moonlight. Mr. Beaton's blood. The notion caused bile to rise in my throat. The trees surrounding the graveyard seemed to lean in, reaching towards the witches as if drawn to their dark energy.

As the chant grew louder, the candle's flame began to twist and spiral, forming a vortex of darkness at its center. The earth trembled, and a cold wind whipped through the graveyard, carrying whispers of forgotten souls. The ritual was reaching its peak, the power of the witches converging to tear open the veil between worlds.

In this moment, the graveyard was no longer a place of rest for the dead but a battleground for ancient forces, with the three women standing at the epicenter, their power and intent as clear as the full moon above.

I cast one final look at Edgar before launching myself into the grove, bursting into the circle and shattering the witches' connection.

I threw myself between Isobel and Angus, and the sudden break in connection caused the candle's flame to flicker violently. The witches turned to face us, their eyes blazing with fury.

"Stop them!" Isobel hissed.

Angus lunged at me, the spell's power crackling in the air, creating an electric intensity that buzzed around us. Edgar grappled with Iona, their bodies a blur of movement as they struggled for control.

My heart pounded in my ears as I fought twisting and turning, my muscles straining as I wrestled the witch to the ground. Angus's nails clawed at my skin, but I held firm, determined not to let go. The ground beneath us trembled.

"Lilian, get back!" Edgar shouted, feeling the vibrations beneath his feet. He grabbed my arm and pulled me to the perimeter of the circle.

"What do we do?" said Edgar as he scanned the grove for a way out of the madness.

I searched the tree line for an escape and then I saw it—a group of grave diggers, shovels on shoulders, in the far corner of the kirkyard had looked toward us. Their eyes widened as they took in the scene.

"Witchcraft! They're casting a dark spell!" I screamed at the top of my lungs. "Help us, PLEASE!"

The diggers dropped their shovels and began weaving between the graves in our direction.

The three witches froze in place, casting terrified glances at each other.

"Isobel, what do we do?" panicked Angus.

"Change of plans," said Isobel. "We are leaving." She held the spellbook over her head and began the familiar weaving movements from the Temple.

"They're trying to move themselves through time, that's the same spell from before," Edgar croaked.

Without hesitation I lunged for Isobel, tackling her at the waist and prying the book from her hands. She howled and clawed at me as a vortex of blackness appeared at the center of their circle. Isobel's voice rose above the din and I clasped a hand over her mouth to silence her incantation.

We grappled on the ground until I had rolled her a safe distance from the growing darkness.

"The men are coming," said Angus, her voice so sharp it could cut glass. "I... I'm sorry Isobel. I can't live that hell again, it was excruciating." She turned her back on her friends and fled.

"Me too. I was enjoying my peaceful life." said Iona turning to flee. In one fluid motion Edgar reached out and ceased her by the wrist.

"I don't think so," he growled. "You'll pay for your betrayal of Mr. Beaton. He was a good man and he loved you." His eyes were fierce and burning.

"I know he did," said Iona. "You don't understand." She pulled at his fingers to free herself but he held her firm.

The voices were closer now, and the magic of the spell was waning. My mind raced with images of Edgar, of his tender words and his willingness to do whatever he could to support me. When the men came, they would certainly seize the book and Edgar and I would be doomed to this timeline.

I knew what I had to do. I released Isobel, who lay in a heap panting, and moved toward Edgar with slow, even steps.

"Lilian!" Edgar's voice pierced through the madness. "What the hell are you doing? Grab her, she's going to escape!"

"It's okay," I said, my voice faltering, the words scratching at my dry throat. I looked directly at Edgar, and in that fleeting moment, a thousand unspoken words passed between us. I reached out, wrapping one arm around his neck, lifted my face to his, and placed a gentle kiss on the surface of his lips. They were so very warm and as soft as I had always imagined. My fingers, trembling but determined, slipped the small book I had pried from Isobel's hands into his pocket. Then I pulled back and shoved him hard in the stomach.

He gasped, the sound piercing through the chaotic air. The look of shock and betrayal in his eyes cut through me like a knife and his mouth fell open, unable to form words. He stumbled, lost his footing, and dragged himself and Iona directly into the path of the swirling energy. The force of the spell caught hold of them, drawing them into the abyss. The air around us hummed with a malevolent energy as his free hand clawed at the air, desperately trying to grab onto me.

"I love you too, Edgar," I yelled, my voice breaking with anguish, each word feeling like it was tearing from my throat.

His form twisted and distorted under the monstrous force, the scene blurring through my tears. My limbs became jelly and my knees buckled. Isobel rose to her feet and towered over me, her eyes blazing with a fiery intensity that scorched my insides.

"Looks like you're in trouble now," she sneered. With one swift movement she brought her knobbly foot up and kicked me hard in the shoulder. I landed hard, the cold, damp earth pressing against my skin. Then she fled into the darkness, disappearing like a wisp of smoke.

I sat alone, the eerie silence of the night broken only by the approaching shouts of the men with torches. Their cries of "Witch!" rebounded through the graveyard. I should have been afraid, but instead, I was overcome with a grim acceptance.. After what I did to Iona, after hurting Edgar, after putting Mr. Beaton in danger—maybe this is what I deserved.

The approaching mob was now close enough that the flickering torchlight cast grotesque patterns on their faces. Their eyes glowed with feral intensity, and their breaths formed visible puffs in the cold night air. I lifted myself onto my knees, my shoulders sagging under the invisible burden of my choices. Each movement felt sluggish, as if thick mud clung to my limbs. I placed my hands behind my head in a gesture of surrender, the cold, damp earth beneath me a final, cruel anchor to this timeline.

The men surrounded me. I could feel the hatred seeping from their pores, a palpable heat radiating from their bodies. The irony of my situation was not lost on me—after immersing myself in the history and intricacies of this era, I now faced the same fate I had read about countless times.

I smiled, not my small usual smile, but a wild, toothy, maniacal grin. I raised my face to the moon and screamed, the sound echoing through the grove, mingling with the distant cries of nocturnal creatures.

Whatever fate awaited me—Edgar is free. I had saved him, given him a chance to escape this nightmare, even if it meant sacrificing myself. For once in my life, I had done the right thing. And in the face of the unknown, that certainty was enough to give me strength.

Chapter Twenty-Eight

Edgar

I jolted awake to the clangor of city traffic, blaring horns and distant sirens pulling me from the darkness. The beeps and honks of modernity felt alien and unknown, a stark contrast to the subdued sounds of the dark ages I had just left behind. The replay of the last few days flashed through my mind, causing me to bolt upright.

"Lilian!" I yelled into the night, my eyes squinting from the burn of artificial light projected down on me from the towering streetlamps.

I searched around me, my head swiveling in all directions. "Lilian… I… I need you," I whimpered.

This time there was no response.

I fell back to the ground and clutched at my chest as the haunting memory of Lilian on her knees, with her hands cradling her head in surrender, flooded me.

In the recesses of my mind, I could hear her final call, "*I love you too, Edgar.*" Her absence descended over me like a heavy fog, the hollowness of life without Lilian dawning on me like the end of days.

My fingers brushed my lips, tracing their edges, the prickle of her kiss still tingling on my skin. Lilian loves me. She had kissed me, and in the end, she had sacrificed herself for me. The ache in me was unbearable. How cruel is the world when just as love is realized, it is stripped away without mercy. My happy ending was gone. I would not grow old in the comfort of Lilian's solitary existence. I was alone, with nothing but the final fleeting memory of her, encircled by enraged men, and the haunting echo of "witch" ringing through the darkness. What would become of her? What fate awaited her? A woman like her, so quick-witted and unrelenting, would surely meet the stake, and swiftly.

Grief consumed me, wrapping its cold, clammy arms around me in a smothering embrace. The memory of Lilian's final moments and her sacrifice played over and over in my mind on a cruel and endless loop. I was being suffocated by the emptiness she left behind, each breath a struggle against the wholeness of my loss.

Suddenly, the dam holding back my emotions broke, and I screamed into the night. The guttural sound barely registered amongst the overwhelming sounds of the city. My face contorted as I clawed at it, trying to block out the images of her. I pounded with clenched fists on the sides of my skull, begging my brain to release me from my torment.

Amid my despair, a thought broke through—the gentle whisper of Lilian moments before the blackness consumed me. "*It's okay*," she had whispered, pulling me close. I had been so entranced by her lips meeting mine that I had missed a key detail of that moment—she slipped something into my pocket.

With shaky hands, I reached into my trousers and pulled out the spellbook. I gasped.

The book in my hands was a tangible connection to Lilian, a lifeline to a hope I had nearly abandoned. The worn leather cover, the ancient pages filled with cryptic symbols and arcane knowledge—it all felt like a gift from her, a final act of love and trust. If I could master the spell within these pages, I could bring Lilian home to me.

My fingers traced the intricate patterns on the cover, feeling the grooves and ridges worn smooth by time. Each symbol pulsed with power, a promise of possibilities yet to be unlocked. The scent of old parchment and ink hit my nostrils and reminded me of her.

I flipped through the pages, each one a gateway to another world, brimming with incantations and diagrams that spoke of times long past. The language was archaic, the script delicate and precise. It would take all my concentration and skill to decipher it, but I was driven by a force stronger than any challenge—my love for Lilian.

Every word, every page felt like a thread weaving a tapestry of hope. I imagined the moment I would see her again, her eyes filled with the same determination and love that had driven her to sacrifice herself. The thought of her smile, her touch, her presence was enough to steady my shaking hands.

I took a deep breath, my resolve hardening. The noise of the modern world faded into the background, replaced by the rhythmic beating of my heart. This book was my key, my guide, and my beacon. I would study every page, master every spell, and harness the power within these secret texts.

For Lilian, I would defy time itself. I would bring her home, no matter the cost.

AFTERWORD

For those finishing the story of Lilian and Edgar there may be a lingering question.

With all of Lilian's oddities and rituals. Is she neuro-divergent? and the short answer is yes.

As a late-diagnosed autistic woman, I often found company between the covers of books. When the world felt lonely and confusing stories of perseverance always gave me hope, but there was one thing that was missing - a character like me.

For much of my life – before my diagnosis I always thought of myself as "weird." Many of the terms used in the book to describe Lilian and her behaviors are both real behaviors I exhibit and words that have been used to describe me, and while it is important to note that the autistic experience is different for every single individual who lives it, it is my hope that those who have struggled to find their place in the world due to a lack of understanding of autism may find in Lilian a glimmer of themselves.

While this is a work of fiction – the hope is that it sheds light on the diverse experiences of neurodivergent people, celebrating their unique perspectives and resilience and recognizing the potential that lies in each of us.

By embracing this story, you have helped to forge a more inclusive future, one where every person, can find their rightful place in the world of literature.

Thank you for reading,

-     L